A
SEASON OF
WHISPERS

A SEASON OF WHISPERS
© 2020 Jackson Kuhl

www.aurelialeo.com

Kuhl, Jackson.
A SEASON OF WHISPERS / by Jackson Kuhl 1st. ed.

ISBN-13: 978-1-946024-82-4 (ebook)
ISBN-13: 978-1-946024-83-1 (paperback)
Library of Congress Control Number: 2020932004

Editing by Lesley Sabga
Cover design by The Cover Collection
Book design by Samuel Marzioli | marzioli.blogspot.com

Printed in the United States of America
First Edition:
10 9 8 7 6 5 4 3 2 1

For James

PRAISE

"With a heart of mystery, a temperament of horror, and a persuasion of literary splendor, Jackson Kuhl's *A Season of Whispers* will lead you though slowly darkening twists until you've sunk inescapably into the sinister depths of Bonaventure Farm."

— *Eric J. Guignard*, *award-winning author and editor, including* That Which Grows Wild *and* Doorways to the Deadeye

"Channeling past masters of the Gothic—namely Hawthorne, Lovecraft, and Poe—Jackson Kuhl has fashioned a pitch-perfect narrative for which those scriveners would be proud."

— *C.M. Muller*, *editor and publisher of* Nightscript

"The monstrous forces that manipulate the Bonaventure commune are surpassed only by the evil that lingers at the heart of humanity: greed, power, and madness. By reaching into America's transcendentalist history, Kuhl has authored a novel that is strangely reflective of our modern world."

— *Marc E. Fitch*, *author of* Boy in the Box *and* Paradise Burns

"*A Season of Whispers* is as much a fascinating tour of an obscure Emersonian outpost in New England as it is a chilling tale of the darkness of a man's soul."

— *Daniel Altiere*, *screenwriter of* Scooby-Doo! The Mystery Begins *and* Scooby-Doo! Curse of the Lake Monster

"In the woods too, a man casts off his years, as the snake his slough."

—Ralph Waldo Emerson, "Nature"

CHAPTER ONE

There is an indescribable sense of satisfaction, known only to a few, in committing a murder and escaping its punishment. We nod in thankfulness as the newspaper tells us about the arrest of some strangler or alleyway knife-man; we mutter to ourselves that justice has been served when we learn how the malefactor was marched up to the platform or thrown into a penitentiary cell. This is easier than the alternative, which is to consider in the recesses of our imaginations the number of villains who have *not* been arrested, who have *not* been executed or imprisoned. We assure ourselves they are fictitious or at least number a small minority simply because we assume a criminal can be identified by marks and tells. Yet nobody is truly familiar with his neighbor, nor can he account for every minute in a beloved spouse's day; and while we suppose we know the life stories of our fathers and grandfathers, we can place no reliance in what transpired during the years before we departed our mothers. No, it is better to recognize that outlaws' whirl around us in the streets and parlors. By definition the murder is perfect because everyone adjacent to the killer is blind and deaf to it.

Tom Lyman had no sooner hopped from the wagon's seat and grabbed hold of his pair of bags than the driver, a taciturn farmer who had granted Lyman a ride from town, flicked the reins and wobbled on without good-bye or acknowledgment. For a moment Lyman stood dejected, bag in each hand, by turns watching the wagon recede and staring up at the old farmhouse. It loomed over him, a commitment made solid in whitewash and cedar shake, and Lyman's gaze rotated between the two, between going forward or back. Once the wagon vanished and only a single course remained to him, Lyman stepped toward the stairs to knock at the front door.

Just then a man walked around the corner of the wide porch. He was dressed in shirtsleeves rolled up to his elbows, with a linen handkerchief tied around his bald scalp to catch an abundance of sweat. When he saw Lyman, his eyes lit up and a smile ruptured his thick beard.

"Mr. Lyman!" he said. "You've made it by hook and crook all the way from Norwalk." He approached and offered a grubby hand. "I am David Grosvenor, your correspondent."

Lyman regarded the extended palm, dirt caked beneath the nails and shading every line and whorl. Or at least he hoped it was dirt; though Lyman knew him to be a lawyer by profession, Grosvenor smelled of manure. But there and then Lyman acknowledged the lack of retreat from the road selected, for had he wanted a diversion from robust living there were countless byways and highways he could have chosen in the weeks prior, before his epistolary exchange with the other man.

He dropped a bag and grasped Grosvenor's hand. "I'm so thankful for your generosity, sir, in having me."

His host laughed and clapped him on the shoulder. "There are no *sirs* or *madams* at Bonaventure Farm, Mr. Lyman—only brothers and sisters. Come inside and we'll get you settled."

For all his resolve, as Grosvenor turned away toward the door Lyman could not help glance in disgust at the dust and grime deposited on the shoulder of his coat by Grosvenor's free hand.

They did not loiter long inside; instead passing through the kitchen where labored several women, including Mrs. Grosvenor, to her husband's small office. There Grosvenor produced a ledger and Lyman, as per their agreed arrangement, laid down five twenty-dollar bills from his wallet. Grosvenor recorded the transaction in his book.

"You now own a full share in our enterprise," said Grosvenor, congratulating the newest member of the co-operative. "Rest assured the money will be put to good use, for improvements and equipment." He tore off a receipt and handed it to Lyman. "In return you are eligible to all privileges and profits achieved by our communal efforts, including lodging and a guaranteed fixed dividend."

"I hope that involves supper daily."

"It does indeed! And breakfast and dinner besides. Now—leave your bags and I will show you the special project I mentioned in my letters."

Lyman stiffened. "Why should I leave my bags here at this house? I imagined I would take up residency immediately in the other."

Grosvenor shook his head. "You have not seen that house, Mr. Lyman. It requires significant work before it is livable."

"But I thought you said there wasn't room elsewhere? That all the beds here in the main house and in the cabins were spoken for." Lyman suddenly suspected Grosvenor meant for him to sleep in a hay loft.

"That's true. But as I told you, our intent is for the stone house to ultimately function as a men's dormitory. When it is restored, the unmarried women of the farm—they sleep upstairs in this house, several to a bed—will emigrate to the cabins, which are currently populated by the farm's bachelors."

"Where will I sleep in the meantime?"

"Until then I'm sorry to say the best we can offer is a couch and a blanket in the parlor. But! Having read in your letters of your considerable skill in carpentry, I imagine the restoration will take a few weeks at most, upon which the ladies will migrate to their new homes and you can join the men in the stone house."

An unease stirred Lyman's abdomen and he regarded Grosvenor, who in that moment resembled another in his mind's eye, with a strange and near-malicious light. The thought of living with a bunch of uncouth and smelly farm hands revolted him; he would have to use whatever influence he could accrue to move in with Grosvenor and his family in the main house. "If it's all the same to you," he said, "allow me to look over the house before passing judgment. Perhaps the assessment of my experienced eye won't be as dire as yours? Assuming so, I may even sleep there tonight."

Grosvenor shrugged. "Suit yourself."

Lyman's host—now his coworker and comrade—led him through the kitchen, and after a brief introduction to his wife, out the back door and between the barn and various sheds and outbuildings to a double-rutted road. They set off along this following a horse fence, and as they walked, Grosvenor the tour guide pointed out the contents of various fields, green and full in the late summer, where men hoed and weeded. The most common of these plantings were potatoes and corn and onions, the latter grown mostly as a cash crop in support of their community.

"Though I do hope you like onions," said Grosvenor, "because the corn has been terribly wormy this year and by February, I assure you, another plate of potatoes on the table will be an almost unbearable sight."

Lyman indicated a pen and shed opposite the fields. "And the hogs?"

"Again, largely for market. Though we eat what bacon we can spare."

"All this food and yet you sound as if you starve."

"We do not starve, Mr. Lyman. It is just that the cost of operations has—well." He stopped himself. "In any event, I will be glad to see the old stone house be put right so that we can invite more young women to join our experiment. We have had a great imbalance of male applicants who seem attracted to Bonaventure mainly by some of, ah, Monsieur Fourier's more *French* ideas, shall we say. Mrs. Grosvenor has been adamant since day one that for Bonaventure to shine as an example to the world, the labor and contributions of both men and women must be perceived as equally worthy—but in order to do so, we must have equal numbers of men and women themselves. Otherwise any success we achieve will be attributed to that imbalance."

A spur led off from the main road. On either side of this cul-de-sac, eight single-room cabins faced each other beneath leafy branches, the maple logs of their walls blond and bright.

"We had the cabins built with capital leftover from the sum used to buy the property. Alas for you, room in neither inn nor manger there."

"I take it those are the bachelors' quarters."

"Seven of them. The last is inhabited by the Albys, a married couple and their young daughter."

"You had money remaining after the sale? So the cost was less than expected?"

"I was able to negotiate a lower price, yes. The farm had been abandoned for more than half a century. The estate was eager to sell. With the remaining difference we were able to make repairs to the main house—which we call the Consulate, by the way—and to build the cabins and buy some equipment."

"Estate?"

"The estate of the Garrick family. They were the original settlers of the area, sometime in the late sixteen-hundreds during the Restoration era. They came over from Dunwich—the *old* Dunwich, in England. A rather large city at one time, I believe, until it fell into the sea, or the sea fell onto it, I suppose. An ancient family much reduced. There was some scandal, so the stories say, some accusation of witchcraft or paganism centering around the familial patriarch—you know how it must have been in those days, Charles the Second back on the throne and all the knives unsheathed, settling grievances real or otherwise. So the Garricks had to flee their ancestral homeland for more salubrious shores. The stone house where I am taking you was their original dwelling until later, when the younger generations built other houses around the property and left the first to the grandfather. He lived to a ripe old age and then some. But their misfortune followed the family from Britain, it seems; the members expired one by one, or moved away, and finally the last Garrick died out west somewhere and the attorneys had to wait fifty years to close accounts and collect their fee."

By now the grass growing along the sides of the road and in the median between the ruts had grown long enough to brush against their calves, while the ruts themselves faded. They had walked half a mile, the road curving gently to their left, before entering a shallow wood that appeared on the right hand. Lyman had a definite impression this land had been cleared at one time—they passed between the bookends of a low tumbledown wall—before springing up again, by slow saplings and creepers, to reconquer its stolen territory. In the shade of the trees the road became sandy and the grass subsided. Then the ground inclined slightly and at the top squatted a house of fieldstone blocks chinked with sand daub. It was a saltbox, its wooden roof sloping from a height of two stories at its centerline to one story in the back. Much of the roof was buried beneath leaves and sticks and branches, and part of it had cratered into the kitchen.

"Here we are," he said. "Doesn't look like someone's been in the house since I last visited."

To this Grosvenor added little, perhaps worried Lyman might reject the project, and they ducked their heads under the lintel of the heavy door frame to tour inside; the thick door, though sticky, was unlocked. The ceilings were higher than Lyman had imagined— "Apparently the elder Garrick was quite tall and thin," Grosvenor said—and the stone kept the air damp but cool. It would be refreshing to live here in the summer months, Lyman reasoned, after one had lit a fire to dry the place. The fireplaces were massive, of course. But it would also be freezing in the winter—which was all the more reason for him to expedite repairs and decamp for the main house. They walked from room to room. Berms of mortar, dissolved into dust, lay at the base of every wall, creating gaps between the stones. The windows were narrow but the glass, with two exceptions, was intact; and the doors, though most without hinges and latches, stood propped beside their frames, waiting to be rehung. Leaves and twigs and nests of a menagerie's worth of varmints lay in the corners or were stuffed among the rafters, though prodding with toe or stick hinted that none seemed to be presently inhabited.

"Mr. Grosvenor," said Lyman, "you have greatly exaggerated the condition of this house."

Grosvenor looked at him with some anxiety.

"I don't see why I can't take occupancy immediately. Some sweeping, reglazing of the panes, reattachment of hardware—the work of a few days. Repointing the walls and the roof will take longer, and a new sanitation pit must be dug, and to prevent further stavings, many of the trees and saplings around the house should be cut down. But these are straightforward tasks. I believe the young men could settle here before the last red leaf has fallen."

Grosvenor beamed. "I knew from your letters you were the right man for the job, Mr. Lyman." He shook Lyman's hand heartily and Lyman, for the first time since arrival, carefully set down the bag in his left hand and sealed their bargain by clasping his palm over their mutual grip.

Later Grosvenor arranged for some men to drive a cart full of supplies down to the house: lamps and lanterns and oil, a broom, a hammer and some hooks, a few dishes and cups and a pot and a pair of fire dogs, firewood, a water jug and a bucket and rope for the well, an old bedstead they wrestled out of the attic of the so-called Consulate, a mattress stuffed with fresh straw, a blanket, a wobbly dresser, and a lunch of cold ham and onions on bread. Lyman spent the rest of the day cleaning and sorting, and he claimed a bedroom for his own based on the size of the hearth rather the room itself. The fire, once lit, did as predicted and chased away the damp. In the late afternoon an exhausted Lyman paused his chores to sit on the edge of the bed, studying the flames; soon he lay back, his eyelids heavy, and dropped his chin to his chest.

He awoke engulfed in darkness. Stumbling through his mnemonic geography he managed to raise the fire and find and light a lamp. Outside lay impenetrable black and chirping frogs and crickets; Lyman had no conception of the hour but judged he had missed supper at the main house. Resolution would have to abide his stomach until daybreak. He poured himself some water from the jug and washed his face and hands and unpacked his clothes into the dresser. The other bag he stuffed under the bed. With log and poker Lyman built up the fire as high as it would safely go and sat staring at it, and gradually a snowfall of calm gathered in his hair and upon his shoulders, an accumulation of peace he hadn't known for weeks. Finally he was secure: ensphered in a globe of night on the edges of civilization, as isolated as a Sandwich Island maroon, but not so alone as to be lonely. The purest bred hound, raised on a diet of nothing except dirty stockings and pinpricks of blood on grass, could not track his footsteps from New York to the little stone ruin perched on the periphery of Connecticut wilderness. He wrapped the blanket around his shoulders and dozed again.

The second time he woke to the sound of a violin. He couldn't have been long asleep. the fire burned brightly; but the night beyond the house had gone silent, with only the scraping of the bow across strings. Lyman lay there a long time, icy needles stabbing him, wondering where the music originated. There was no wind to carry it from the house or some other building. Maybe someone fiddled while walking along the road? An approaching visitor. Then the playing, mournful at first, kicked up to a merry jig, and Lyman jumped to raise the lamp wick and push on his shoes.

He followed the sound from the bedroom to the stairs and descended. It was louder on the first floor, seeming to rise from the boards rather than out-of-doors. When he reached the basement door, it abruptly cut off.

It so happened that the basement door at the top of the worn stone steps, along with the front and kitchen doors, had not been stripped of its iron and thus functioned as intended. Additionally—and Lyman hadn't thought this odd in the daylight, but now wasn't so sure—the door was fitted with a crossbar, which, as there was no direct entrance from outside to the basement, seemed unnecessary.

He undid the bar, opened the door, held the lamp high. Nothing but shadow—the light failed to reach the floor below. Neither glimmer of light nor sounding of fiddle note wafted from the darkness.

The flame of the lamp leaned and flickered. Air brushed the hairs of his short beard: a breeze on his face. Something moved toward him at fast speed he realized, something large, its mass pushing the air ahead of it. Even now it noiselessly rushed up the stairs at him.

Lyman slammed the door, shot the bar through its cleat, threw his weight against the wood—steeled himself for the impact against the other side.

None came. After a long moment he looked at his lamp. The flame stood straight as a soldier.

He took a deep breath. Upon returning to his room it didn't take him long to convince himself he had imagined everything, that the only music had been the cotton of a dream clinging to his sleepy skull. He tossed another log on the fire and lay back on the mattress, listening as the usual players outside again took up their instruments and played him off to sleep.

In winter or rain, Lyman was told, meals were served indoors with every member sitting cheek by jowl; but because the morning was warm and dry, breakfast was like a picnic on July Fourth, served under an elm in the Consulate's yard on battered tables with old linens and mismatched chairs. Hungry as he was, Lyman hesitated as he approached the band of men already established at the motley furnishings, gossiping as they awaited the meal's arrival. Their trousers were striped, their waistcoats checked, and their frock coats the best offered by the shops of Providence or New London; but Lyman observed here and there the worn sleeves and frayed hems of good clothes put to hard use, and most of all he noted the sweat stains on every man's cravat. Each fellow had removed and set nearby his hat—or, in some cases, used his to fan away the flies—all of which were specimens of the wide-brimmed style of the countryman rather than the tall, narrow-ledged trend of the metropolitan. Their faces, whether voluble or unforthcoming as they chatted, had none of the craggy dourness one expects of men accustomed to toil but instead bespoke of softer and more gracile origins, suggesting childhoods spent in fine homes rather than in fields and of lessons learned in heated schoolrooms rather than in frigid barns or henhouses.

Just then Grosvenor noticed him and, after a series of introductions which pelted Lyman like the drops of a rain shower, each name too fast and insubstantial to catch, he was warmly invited to sit; when Lyman explained why he had missed supper, Grosvenor scolded himself for not checking on him before nightfall.

"Your exhaustion is completely understandable," said Grosvenor. "The travel, then a full day's work just so you could sit down and make a fire. Anyone would have done the same."

A stream of women, their side curls bouncing, poured out of the kitchen door carrying platters of grits and butter and bread and jam and bacon and boiled eggs, spreading them among the tables before joining the seated men. When the most beautiful of the cooks plopped down next to Lyman, he struggled whether to rise—she being a lady and he a gentleman, and yet their experiment demanded tradition be overturned—and instead invoked a half-crouched position that seemed more apt for the outhouse than the breakfast table. She laughed.

"This is the immediate dilemma, Mr. Lyman," she said. "Which customs to keep and which to throw away as regressive? I can see neither benefit nor detriment to your standing while I sit—at least from my perspective."

"Into the trough with it then," said Lyman, attempting to recover some measure of poise, "but what about the lady folk preparing the meals and the men working the fields? Isn't that division of labor among the chief problems we seek to revolutionize?"

"Agreed. But we each bring to Bonaventure the skills learned in the old mode—you have your carpentry, for example. Unfortunately, most men today are so poorly schooled that they can contribute little but the simplest brute labor, whereas we women can knit, cook, weed, and slop the pigs in equal proficiency. If the men dining alongside us right now were to do the cooking, we'd all starve by Monday. The key to reform is to teach our sons and daughters to bake and darn and sow and reap equally, regardless of sex."

Lyman nodded. "I should like to raise such sons and daughters with you," he said, and immediately wished he hadn't.

But she laughed again and offered her hand. "Introductions first, if you please, Mr. Lyman. I'm Minerva."

Her full name, it turned out, was Minerva Katherine Grosvenor, the only child of the commune's founders. Raised by such a pair of reformers she was perhaps more evangelical than the parents; but through some mysterious distillation of rearing had none of the seriousness of the zealot and all the good humor of a missionary among hopeless cannibals. Their cause, she understood, was Sisyphean from onset and therefore no excuse for pessimism and temper. She was, in no particular order, an obsessive reader of *The Dial*, fond of strolling the countryside over sitting in a sewing room, and the possessor of tanned arms and brown eyes that sparkled when she smiled, which was often.

Lyman was smitten.

"We should send down a rooster to the stone house so you don't miss any more meals," Minerva said. "City people think they only crow at dawn but the truth is they crow morning, noon, and night as it suits them. You will never oversleep again."

This talk of sound reminded Lyman of something, and he addressed Minerva's father, sitting to her far side. Lyman had, while walking that morning to breakfast on the road not far from the stone house, been stopped in his tracks by several sharp retorts not unlike artillery or fireworks, followed by a low rumble rolling over the trees and fields that vibrated the ground itself. It was very different from thunder, which surrounds and envelops the listener from above, he said; this was more like a slow shallow wave on the outgoing tide, seething toward him from a specific direction roughly to the north and west. Lyman asked if there was a powder house nearby—for surely the whole thing had just gone up at a spark, though he never saw smoke or flame.

"You truly are a newcomer to the area," said Grosvenor. "Those, Mr. Lyman, are known as the Moodus Noises. They have nothing to do with gunpowder; rather they are a naturally occurring phenomenon unrelated to thunder. Reports date back to the earliest settlers."

"What in nature could produce so loud a noise but not be thunder?"

"Ah, now we have struck upon a favorite pastime of mine: geology."

Grosvenor wiped his mouth with his napkin and leaned toward Lyman. "The noises usually occur with regularity—often in the early morning, as you have discovered, or at dusk. There are several competing theories. The first supposes there are various mineral deposits that mix to form a kind of naturally occurring black powder underground which occasionally detonates, but I find this too improbable. Another hypothesizes gases are to blame. This is more likely but alone is incomplete. Where then do the gases originate? I suspect volcanic activity may be the source. Undoubtedly underground hot springs and geysers, which are known to erupt with great predictability."

"Then where is the sulfur and brimstone?" asked his daughter. "Where is the hot water? It would save me the trouble of having to boil some on the stove for my bath."

"It is kept entirely subterranean, dearest. By the time it feeds into our streams it is already cold."

Lyman frowned. "But what of the fumes? I visited the springs at Saratoga once. Even the more temperate examples are evident by the plumes of steam and calcification of minerals on the earth around them."

Minerva said, "Not to mention such a theory fails to explain the sinkholes that exist on the property, as we've learned." A strange shadow crossed her face.

Grosvenor chewed his lip and tapped his finger against his cup, for in truth he had already recognized these nuisances to his theory. "You know, Mr. Lyman, one of the goals of Bonaventure is to demonstrate that labor and self-sufficiency do not preclude furtherance of the arts and sciences, and that working to feed oneself and his community doesn't necessitate ignorance. After all, doesn't Mr. Emerson himself state that all science has but one aim, which is to discover a theory of nature? Perhaps you would like to assist me in my inquiries. It is a lot to ask, I realize—the spare minutes of your day are already few enough as is."

Lyman looked to Minerva. She smiled.

"I'd be delighted."

Grosvenor slapped the table. "Excellent! Now tell me, what do you know of *fossils?*"

Supplies arrived at the stone house. A stack of planks from the mill, a bucket of nails and tools from the smith. Lyman set about doing what he could, glad no one else was around to witness his trials. He had, in his letters to Grosvenor, mildly exaggerated his talents as a carpenter insofar as he had never before held a hammer in hand, let alone an ax. Having read about Bonaventure Farm in a newspaper at the Norwalk coffeehouse where he had taken to lurking, Lyman conceived that a winter in the wilds of eastern Connecticut would obscure his tracks completely. He immediately rattled off a letter to the farm's master praising the experiment. Grosvenor responded kindly, and after another round of correspondence, Lyman obliquely sounded the depths for what skills were most in demand. When Grosvenor mentioned a certain enigmatic endeavor called for a carpenter's deft touch, Lyman painted an appropriate self-portrait. He had assured himself at the time, as he dipped pen into pot, that woodworking could be easily learned in the field—whatever promises necessary to achieve his end could be fulfilled, *would* be fulfilled, once there. A week later came the offer of employment, an invitation to exhibit to the world what tomorrow would resemble.

The road begun in midsummer now found Lyman scuttling about the back roof, orbiting the hole blasted clean through the shingles by a fallen branch, clearing debris and gingerly removing rotten boards to assess what must be done. To say he did so calmly or without a rising sense of anxiety over the warranties made by his letter-writing self would be incorrect. The roof, to his eye, seemed like a Chinese puzzle dropped by a clumsy child, then thrust at him to fix. He slipped, he stumbled, he rolled off once, badly bruising his ribs and shoulder, and on a separate occasion was left hanging when the makeshift stairway he had made of rocks and sticks, as stable as the skin on a bowl of soup, collapsed beneath him. When his plea up at the Consulate for a ladder was met with shrugs, in frustration he took the ax and with skinned knuckles, cut rails and rungs from saplings, bored the holes with the drill that had arrived with the rest of the tools, and pounded it all together. Only after it supported his weight, granting a wobbly passage skyward without accident, did the steam of his temper at the earlier Lyman ease by a modicum.

Yet it was another preoccupation of Lyman's that hindered progress at the stone house. The experience of the first night had never been repeated. Often, on the edge of sleep, he wondered if he had imagined the music; in the daylight the answer was unequivocal, but in the night less so. Then there had been the air blowing on his face, which suggested subterranean currents—perhaps caused by the springs Grosvenor had conjectured. So, against instinct, he lit a lantern and ventured down the cellar stairs.

As a rule Lyman avoided basements for the same reasons he avoided manual labor, for both involved dirt and stains and unfortunate surprises such as cobwebs across his face. The basement of the stone house was deeper than he had imagined, with abundant room between pate and rafter, and here and there a few streams of sunlight cascaded down from cracks in the floorboards. He paced the rectangle of the fieldstone foundation from the stairway around again, holding his lantern up to widen the circle of vision, but finding nothing of interest beyond an old crate and a clump of rags in a corner where long ago a rat had made its nest.

Dry as a chicken bone, the air musty and dense, no sign of Styx, no sniff of sulfur. The fiddle music had been his brain, Lyman accepted; being unaccustomed to the quiet of the woods, his mind had filled the emptiness with tavern noise. The breeze on his beard had probably been the wind outside, flowing through the roof hole then down between the floorboard cracks and up the stairs again in a sinuous stream. The only bogeyman in the house was Lyman, him and his too many years of city living.

Yet as he stomped up the stairs, between the gaps created by the absent risers he noted a shadow that did not bounce with the lantern's light. He leaned over the shaky banister. Something there, fixed and stable behind the stairway: an aperture in the stone that swallowed illumination.

He descended again, ducked under the stairs, raised the lantern.

At first an outline, then a recession, then an entrance leading away. A tunnel.

Based on the rough jambs it was not part of the basement's original design; stones had been pulled out of the wall and a lintel inserted over the break. Lyman ducked, holding the lantern ahead of him, shielding himself from the webs and spider husks.

After ten steps the passage widened into a new chamber. Rougher and cruder than the basement, built of smaller stones, and round. Slowly Lyman rose from his tunnel hunch, holding the lamp overhead. He stood inside a dome: the stones fitted together like the blocks of snow in a child's igloo. No one, Lyman believed, had been in the chamber for a long time: most of the iron in the rest of the house had been stripped and yet in the center of the chamber's floor was set a large steel grate. It had been painted at some point, which, while flaked, had prevented it from rusting into a solid unmovable mass.

Lyman held his lantern down to the bars, figuring to see its light reflected in black waters below. When it wasn't, he attempted to lift the grate one-handed, and when this failed, he set the lamp down and attacked it with two.

Once while walking along South Street, Lyman had witnessed a pair of ships collide in the harbor, their sides screaming as they rubbed past each other, the sailors swarming over the rigging and hollering and swearing to murder their brethren on the opposite vessel. Lyman wished the grate was as quiet as that. By bare inches it moved, and Lyman bent his knees and pushed himself standing, bringing it almost vertical— and then not. It slammed backwards to the dirt, the pit yawning and open, and for an instant Lyman teetered on the precipice, spinning his arms like whirligigs. But then a puff of gas, hot and rancid, blew up the shaft and pressed against his chest like a flat palm. He stumbled rearwards and away.

The lantern, when Lyman knelt on the edge and tepidly dangled it as far over as he could reach, revealed an iron ladder bolted to the sides of the shaft. At the bottom some ten or twelve feet down, the round mouths of more tunnels gaped at intervals into darkness.

"And there they shall remain, unexplored," Lyman said aloud.

A cistern gone dry. He could conceive no other purpose for the pit, though an amateurish mineshaft wasn't out of the question—maybe Old Man Garrick had come over from England to dig for gold. But here again, as ever since coming to Bonaventure, was an answer to a dilemma.

Lyman left the chamber, returning minutes later with the bag from under his bed. He knotted a double length of twine around its handles, locking it closed, then knotted the ends around a wrought-iron wall hook with a bowline taught to him by a stevedore. Hand over hand he lowered the bag into the pit; and when it reached its end, he clipped the hook onto the top rung of the ladder. The bag and its contents hung suspended in space, deep inside a pit in a secret basement beneath a half-ruined house in the wild Connecticut woods. No one, not even God squinting down from the cumulus, would find the money now.

"Mr. Lyman!"

Lyman jumped. From somewhere unknown a muffled voice, a hundred miles away, followed by thumps on wood. "Mr. Lyman, are you home?"

The front door. Lyman rushed from the chamber, crouched and shuffled through the tunnel, bounded up the stairs. He remembered to blow out the lantern's wick before pulling open the door.

"Mr. Lyman!" said Minerva. "What—why look at you." Lyman tried to steady the heavy breathing of his dash. She reached out to peel a cobweb off his sleeve. "I thought you might be out but now I see you've been hard at work. Down the basement I presume?"

"Ah," said Lyman, "yes, as a matter of fact. Checking the foundation. Very dirty and dusty down there. I cannot recommend it. So I will not invite you to witness it. Or anyone else for that matter. Everyone should stay out. Of the basement, I mean."

"And?"

"And what?"

"The foundation? Is it sound?"

"Oh yes. Yes. Absolutely. Steady as Gibraltar. All the more reason no one should go down there. No point."

Minerva's perplexity was clear but fortunately for Lyman, the two stood in the early stages of infatuation in which any and all idiosyncrasies proved endearing. "Well, considering your situation so isolated from the rest of the farm, I thought it might be nice today if instead of you going to lunch, lunch should go to you." She carried a basket under her arm. "Would now be a good time for a bit of a picnic, Mr. Lyman? If you are too involved in your work, I shouldn't want to bother you —"

"No! I mean—yes," said Lyman, "I mean, no, I'm not too busy and yes, I should very much like to have a picnic with you. Thank you, Miss Grosvenor."

"Oh stop, Tom. Please address me by my given name."

There was a clearing a short distance from the house which the sun, just past noon, bathed in speckled light through the leaves. From her basket Minerva unrolled a blanket and set out a lunch of ham sandwiches and cold boiled potatoes and a jar of sun tea. She poured him a glass.

"So I must ask," she said, "have you met the Devil yet?"

Lyman looked at her. "Whatever do you mean?"

"The Devil. Have you heard him playing his fiddle in your basement?"

Lyman choked on his tea.

"That's the legend, anyway," said Minerva as Lyman hacked and coughed. "Passers-by swear they hear fiddling from the stone house late at night. It's one of the reasons why no one has lived in the house for so long. The whole farm, in fact, is alleged to be haunted. That's why my father was able to pick it up so cheaply."

Lyman wiped his beard and said with a hoarse voice, "He told me it was because the farm was trapped in probate. That the original family, the Garricks, slowly extinguished until there were no more heirs."

"So they did. But did he tell you *how* they extinguished?"

"Well, no."

"Precisely. Because no one knows. They just vanished. Disappeared, one by one. No signs of evil intent among the survivors, just gone. As if they were swallowed into the earth."

"Your father said some of them moved away, that the final Garrick died on the frontier."

"Wouldn't you depart a place if your siblings and parents and assorted relations kept mysteriously popping off into aether?"

Lyman had come to think of Bonaventure as a place to escape *to*, but upon reflection he supposed to others it might be a place to escape *from*. "More to the point: has anyone disappeared at Bonaventure since you moved here?"

"Not so much as an egg from the henhouse."

"Well, there's that. What about the elder Garrick, the one from England? He was said to have lived a long time."

"And died of natural causes, apparently. If it was a family curse, I imagine it was on his wife's side."

"Or he was the one in the larder grinding the rest into sausage."

"Tom! I do like a gentleman who isn't all flowers and rainbows," and she clinked her glass against his. "But I think there's more than one mystery present here at Bonaventure. Namely: you."

With great effort, Lyman kept the muscles of his face relaxed, his expression neutral. With deliberation he set his glass on the blanket and dabbed his mouth with the napkin. "All men contain an infinitude, isn't that what Mr. Emerson tells us? An infinitude of depths, of mysteries and secrets."

"Indeed. And yet in our conversations I'm given the impression that you have come lately to Emerson and philosophy, transcendental or otherwise, and that your passion for our project doesn't burn as hotly as others'. I think you've come to Bonaventure for ulterior purposes. I think you're running away from something and you've come here to hide."

Lyman looked at her steadily. "You're right, Minerva."

"Aha!"

"I am running away."

"Here it comes."

Lyman breathed deeply, steeling himself. He had yet to tell the story to another living soul. "There was a girl—"

"*I knew it.*"

"—a very pretty girl, whom I courted. However, her family

criticized my lack of means —"

"And when you proposed she said *no* and rejected you and full of despair you ran away and now here you are. I knew it!"

"The thing of it is," said Lyman, a bit annoyed at the apparent cliché of his life's story, "was that just before my proposal I inherited a good deal of money from an uncle, which I presented in cash to show to her—"

"To *show off* to her."

"Well, yes. But even that was not enough. She said my inheritance was merely a unique event and questioned how I should support her in a proper manner when that money was gone. I told her I could invest it, grow it. And yet."

"You'll forgive me if I'm happy for her ingratitude, Tom. Had she accepted, you would not be here and the stone house would be as ruinous as ever. As it is, it is much improved."

"Improved? All I've done is sweep the floors and roof."

"More than that. I seem to recall as I knocked on the door seeing a very stout ladder against the wall."

A strange sensation flushed through Lyman, spreading through and to the ends of him, not unlike a glass of whiskey after retreating indoors from a snowstorm.

"I dare say," said Minerva, filling the space, "even Bitty Breadsticks would live at the house now, and she has always avoided it." At Lyman's blank expression, she added, "Bitty Breadsticks is an itinerant traveler, shall we say, who passes through from time to time. Anyway," she said, "all of us at Bonaventure are better for your romantic difficulties."

"And you, Minerva? I should think you'd be in receipt of ten proposals a day. Or does your father chase them off?"

"There *was* one gentleman but when I did not reciprocate his feelings, he quit the farm. He was very earnest, however." For half a moment, Minerva glanced off into the trees in dreamy reminiscence. "As it is, I see no benefit to marriage for a woman beyond the utilitarian, the economy of sharing resources and income and so forth. The odds of finding a true partner—an equal of mind and soul—are so long that it is hardly worth the bother of courtship."

"All the same, people do find such companionship."

"Some people. Maybe so. But right now I'm too busy with Bonaventure, reading and writing and conversing and *changing the world*, to concern myself with a distant hope. I don't forsake weddings and children but I do shepherd my efforts closely."

Neither wanted the picnic to end but clocks and planets turn irrespective of our wishes. They gathered the things into the basket and Lyman snapped the blanket a few times to shake off the leaves and grass before folding it. He started back toward the stone house, then stopped after glancing over his shoulder. Minerva stood frozen by their lunching spot, staring at him.

"Did you feel that?"

Lyman hadn't noticed anything. "Feel what?"

Minerva remained silent, then shook her head. "For an instant I had the oddest sensation the ground moved."

Lyman was in no rush to return to his rooftop tumbling and believed it to be the gentlemanly thing to do, new world or no, to escort Minerva on the walk back to the Consulate. For her part Minerva welcomed his company on the pretext of having set aside some foodstuffs in the kitchen—a sack of apples, some cornmeal and salt and other small things—for Lyman to take with him to the stone house so that he might, if hungry and fatigued, have some refreshment between mealtimes, and also at the very least have a few comestibles lying around in case a visitor again came calling. The pair said their adieus at the kitchen door, and Lyman reembarked for the stone house with the sack slung over his shoulder.

As the kitchen of the stone house was the very room that lacked a roof, Lyman had yet to use it as such. Instead he marched the sack up the stairs to his bedroom, the only comfortable chamber in the house, where he sorted and suspended his rations from hooks while reminiscing about the afternoon.

"*Someone's been in the house.*"

The effect of those five words, spoken from an indistinct point somewhere behind Lyman's right shoulder, was dynamic. Lyman managed, cat-like, to both twist and thrust forward in the same motion, slamming himself into the brick of the fireplace while simultaneously upsetting the apples and spilling the water jug and scattering salt across the boards.

There was nothing behind him. Nothing but air and the rest of the room. And yet he had distinctly heard the words, their sibilance fresh in his right ear as if the speaker had leaned in to whisper them. Lyman was not drowsy; he was neither falling asleep nor waking up. Someone had spoken. Some words had been said. Something had told him—what?

It was at that moment as he stood, breathing hard, surveying the chamber with wild eyes, that he noted the bed was unmade; but Lyman, perhaps from his years as a diligent clerk tallying the contents of storerooms and scrutinizing bills of lading, was fastidious in his habits, never failing to pull the covers square upon rising.

An impulse sent him to the chest of drawers; his clothes and sundries, he could tell, had been disturbed, then put back hastily to mask the disturbance. The bed, he realized, the bed—the bed frame, upon closer scrutiny, had been pulled aside, pushed back into place.

Someone *had* been in the house while he was with Minerva.

His hands fumbled with the lamp wick, his shoes pounded down the basement stairs and swept him through the tunnel. The bag still hung from the top of the ladder; he reeled it up, pulled back its lips. The money was untouched, all of it. It had not been found. Lyman suspected, without any real proof but based upon an odd intuition alone, that the second basement itself had also remained hidden.

Lyman did not go to supper that night at the Consulate. He couldn't bear the thought of leaving only to return, in twilight or full-blown evening, to the darkened house; the anticipation of passing through the front door, exposing himself to every shadow within, terrified him. Instead he sat on the bed, his back wedged into a corner of the room, and slowly gnawed apples picked off the floor. Somewhere, out there, was an enemy, and somewhere closer by was a friend; but their identities or even their natures Lyman could not fathom. The late August night was hot but he kept the fire high anyway, feeding it with logs and apple cores.

Minerva's father pursued his studies in natural philosophy in a fallow pasture far behind the cabins, screened from sight by a line of trees. There, hidden amid the waving stalks of wild grass, lay the partial foundation of a building Lyman had heard the other Bonaventurists reference as either a Phalanstery or a Fraternum or sometimes a Lyceum, a structure that once was a focus of their communal labor but which had been since forgotten and therefore lapsed, for unspecified reasons, into a crepuscular state of earthly return.

The original purpose of the edifice was likewise ambiguous, varying by respondent; but in each interview Lyman detected notes of loss or warmhearted remorse, as if he or she recalled a childhood summer, a whimsical period in a lifetime never to be experienced again. In each reply also the farm itself was implicated in the structure's abandonment, and Lyman was compelled to believe that the two could not coexist.

When the Grosvenors and the initial subscribers settled Bonaventure, they understood beforehand the major tasks involved in farming, the plowing and seeding and weeding and reaping. Yet what they hadn't foreseen were the myriad other chores necessary to farm living. The animals needed feeding, their pens or stables needed mucking. The cows demanded milking, butter required churning, the garden wanted hoeing and attention. As inside, so outside, for as the floors were swept and the beds made, so the grass in the yard must be mowed, rails hand split for the fences, and sundry minor repairs and fixes done to beat back the elemental encroachment of weather and decay. Nor was there any end to washing, to the laundering of clothes and linens, or to the scrubbing of cookware and dishes. Only once these and countless other tasks were affected was there a little time for reading and reflection and the further entertainments of Bonaventure, which were in fact its whole reason for being.

Farming was a distraction that became Bonaventure's profession.

"On a farm," Grosvenor said to the younger Lyman, "animals are frequently butchered. The parts that are unwanted or aren't useful, which are few, end in a refuse pile, and the parts that *are* useful eventually end up there too, or at least the bones do. Keep in mind that successive generations at the farm also have successive heaps; and further, that waste does not always stay where it was last placed—vermin will often drag it hither and yon. I once knew of an elm inhabited by a family of raccoons and the base of it could have been mistaken for a burying ground turned upside down, if drumsticks and soup bones were interred by their widows. Of course, every farm has its dogs and barn cats as well as mice and other rodents, all of whom add their own remains to the soil in good time. And let us not forget horses! The noble steed, the faithful workman, who at last is usually buried where he falls, or at least dragged with effort a not very far distance. Same for oxen."

He thrust a shovel into the earth closest to the hand-laid stones.

"The result, Mr. Lyman, is that to stand within a farm's fence posts is to stand inside a cemetery. Bones, bones, everywhere underfoot, and it takes only a plow's edge or a spade or even a hard rain to unveil to daylight that which was secret. While digging the trench for this foundation," Grosvenor tossed aside a shovel load of dirt, "a few of the other community members and I uncovered some most unusual bones."

He thrust the shovel at Lyman.

"What I would like for you to do is to join the search. In your free time, of course."

Lyman frowned. "You want me to dig a hole?"

"Not dig a hole, no. That would be tedious. I wish for you to find more of the bones like those we've already discovered. Consider it an apprenticeship of sorts."

"I still don't understand the point of the exercise."

"The point is to join me in my study of natural science. To improve Bonaventure, to demonstrate to the outside world that our community is both self-sustaining *and* a center for science and inquiry. The *point*, Mr. Lyman, is that the bones we found are just that—*bones*, and not fossils."

"You're suggesting it's a surprise they should be one and not the other."

Grosvenor said, "'*There are more things in heaven and earth, Horatio, than are dreamt of in your philosophy.*'" And then he chortled at his own literacy.

After long cogitation and for lack of any better strategy, Lyman finally decided to peel back an undamaged section of the stone house's roof. This, he theorized, would provide him with a blueprint useful for repairing the hole over the kitchen; but upon doing so a new problem identified itself. He surmised that a supporting beam, having been broken in the original catastrophe and rotted away, was missing from the damaged area; and in his zeal to clear the space of old wood, Lyman had ripped out any remnant or trace of it, leaving the roof unsupported. It was in poorer shape than when he'd found it.

Lyman lived every waking moment under the weight of a sword dangling overhead, waiting for the hour in which his charades were revealed. Asking Grosvenor or anyone else was to risk questions and ultimate discovery. Whatever the solution to the absent beam, it would have to be his alone. None of the planks supplied to him was thick enough for the replacement. Fine, he thought; he could sister three of them together to make a beam of suitable girth, but he had no worthy fasteners. He looked to his shaky ladder for inspiration. He cut and shaved some straight lengths of sapling into pins, drilled holes through the trio of planks, and doweled them together. But the resulting beam was too heavy for him to lift into place by himself. He would have to hold his breath and request help.

The response at the supper table was contrary to his fear. All marveled at the thrift and ingenuity in constructing the makeshift beam, and Grosvenor repeated his claim that Bonaventure was better for Lyman's arrival. Lyman, glancing across the table at an approving Minerva, saw something in her eyes that made his stomach jump. There was no shortage of volunteers for the task, though Lyman suggested only two men were necessary, and so the following morning after breakfast, a pair returned with him to the stone house.

Their names were Presley and Sutton and they bunked together in one of the cabins close to the Consulate. Lyman found they were in no rush to work; after a cursory tour of the house—which excluded any exploration of the basement—Sutton suggested a pot of tea would strike the right mood for labor, and for a long time the three sat outside on a log with their backs to the stone wall of the house, drinking and gossiping while the first yellow leaves rained down in the cool bright morning. Sutton composed a poem about the turning season, speaking the couplets between five-minute intervals of silence in which he concocted his next lines; and Presley wondered if the sky was best described as sapphire, azure, or cobalt, before settling on a color he had once seen in a painting—a seascape—that he could not identify. Occasionally Lyman would say, "Now about that beam," or slap his thigh and stand up with energy; but all of these gestures at duty were ignored by the other two and eventually Lyman would retake his seat and wait further.

A peculiar thing then happened as the morning progressed and the air warmed. Presley, complaining of the heat, unbuttoned and removed his coat, which he threw over a low branch. His waistcoat soon followed. Then, after a few more tickings of the clock, he gradually undid his shirt, which soon joined the coat and vest, and he sat down on the log beside Lyman bare-chested, doughy as pancake batter and white as a summer flounder having sprouted hair. All the while Sutton, who had given up his poem and begun speaking about pigs both general and specific, observed this behavior narrowly. When Presley stood again and began fumbling with his remaining garments, Sutton leapt up in anger.

"If you touch one button of those trousers, I will box your ears square."

"It is a beautiful day and I am over-warm," said Presley with mildness.

"A more temperate day could not be conceived. You will not disrobe."

"Why, what forbids it? There are no women about, even though it is without shame for either me or them."

Sutton turned to Lyman. "David has insisted Presley here not express his peculiar philosophy in front of the women of Bonaventure and only in the privacy of the cabin. Why such punishment should be inflicted upon me as his house mate, I cannot say. For the most part Presley has obliged though I am afraid poor Mrs. Alby and her daughter has not been entirely unscathed—Presley cavorts about the yard at all hours."

"It does no good to remain indoors. Eden was without log cabins."

"Damn you, Presley."

Lyman observed this revue with ascending alarm, wishing they could just install the beam and return him to his solitude. Presley, however, spoke to Lyman in an evangelical tone.

"Brother Tom," he said with a sincerity rarely seen outside a pulpit, "what if I told you there was a medicine that could cure you of all sickness and disease by preventing it from ever taking root in your blood? What if I told you this medicine gave health and long life and was free of cost and readily available around us? That this medicine was the sun and air itself and has been known to us since the days of Adam? I speak of course, Tom, of the power of *nudism*."

Sutton, with a curse, pounded the log with his fist, and the two men fell to arguing.

This went on for a few minutes until Lyman, realizing there was nothing to do but mediate, brokered a truce in which the benefits of public nakedness were considered and its detriments denied, or at least not disputed for the time being; but that trousers would stay fastened while they worked, regardless of the day's pleasantness.

The incident, at least, had the benefit of finally spurring the men to action.

"You see who and what Bonaventure attracts," Sutton said low to Lyman as they worked on the roof, gesturing with his hammer to Presley's hindside down below. "*Every reform was once a private opinion*, says our august Emerson, and yet these are our reformers: misfits and eccentrics."

"I suppose upon examination every man holds some queer belief or two," said Lyman. "And by its very nature these will bubble to the top of the saucepan at a place like Bonaventure."

Sutton considered. "There's some sense in that. I myself came here out of a wish to separate from a society that condones and abets the evils of slavery and to live among abolitionists only. I refuse to think of that idea as queer, however, or on the same grounds as Presley's dogma. It is the civilization outside the farm that is queer, insofar as it would truck in misery and pain."

"But to them, you and I are the queer ones."

"We are the *correct* ones." He scraped and hammered, preparing for the beam. "And you, Tom? What road led to Bonaventure for you?"

Lyman smiled and shrugged. "Despair at milling table legs and hanging shutters for the gentry. I wanted to help the poor and give my labor meaning so I left Norwalk and came here."

This summation was scene and act from Lyman's epistolary script with Grosvenor, with the *ad libitum* bit about poverty tailored to Sutton's sensibility.

But the quip, intended to encourage fraternity, had the opposite effect. Sutton stopped work and squinted at him. "Your hands are too uncalloused and your carpentry too poor for that story to hold much water."

Lyman's blood froze and he scrambled to assemble a counter-argument. But before he could, Sutton said, "You know, in my former career I was a broker at the Exchange Board on Manhattan. I dealt in cotton and tobacco—in fact, it was exposure to the slave labor behind it that brought me hither. There was a warehouse I had dealings with, quite a large one on South Street, and you bear a strong resemblance to one of the clerks there."

As he had with Minerva during their picnic, Lyman again practiced facial impassivity. "I'm sorry to admit Bonaventure is as far as I've ever roamed from Norwalk."

"You're the very image of that clerk, if I'm not mistaken."

"Should there be a Remus to my Romulus, I've never met him." Lyman tried to laugh but instead sputtered like a crow.

Sutton said nothing but kept at his examination of Lyman until finally, mumbling an excuse, Lyman descended the ladder to earth, where he found the company of the half-naked Presley oddly preferable.

As the days stretched farther into September, Lyman convinced himself the voice he had heard that afternoon in the bedroom—the whispered warning spoken just over his shoulder—had sprung from the well of his imagination alone.

The distance of time and the habit of rationalism rearranged events in his memory; he told himself he had realized the trespasser's presence a split-second before hearing the words, words which only echoed the thoughts flashing that moment through his mind. He only *believed* he'd heard a voice. Those syllables, like the violin of the first night, were nothing but the strange breezes moving under the house and up the dry cistern in the basement, creating whispers and whistles just as breath does across the lip of a flute. The dome shape of the cistern chamber doubtless magnified the sounds. Loud enough, they would've created the illusion of an explosion, like the Moodus Noises did. It was only the blacksmith of the mind that forged the red sounds into recognizable shapes. Nor was Lyman's fancy alone: Minerva had said people had heard fiddling in the stone house for years.

All of it was a distraction from the real question of *who* had been in the house and searched his belongings, and whether his (or even her) goal had been the money or some other inscrutable purpose. After their work together on the roof, Sutton stood tall on the list of possible suspects. Clearly the man doubted Lyman's biography. But Lyman could not disabuse himself of the feeling Sutton had never been to the stone house before that day on the roof; by mannerisms and small indications, he had struck Lyman as a genuine stranger to the scene. Perhaps then the intruder had been another member of the farm. But whom among the more than two dozen?

This line of inquiry soon awoke a cynic within Lyman who suggested that the timing of his absence away from the house may not have been coincidence. Lyman could not imagine Minerva colluding with anyone to deceive him; but the Diogenes on Lyman's shoulder stated his emotions were but rag dolls in her grip. *No*, Lyman insisted. Rather someone had been watching them and used the picnic as the opportunity to enter and rifle the house. Lyman reasoned that if the circumstances of the picnic were duplicated, the culprit might attempt his burglary again, providing a chance for Lyman to catch him *in flagrante*—or at least uncover some clue to his identity.

In sequel to their picnic, Lyman had invited Minerva to walk with him, to which she happily consented. It soon became a standing date where, every other afternoon weather permitting, they would meet at the stone house and explore the woods around it. Lyman often chose the route, planning long circuitous paths that would suddenly cut back into view of the house, where he could observe any disturbance or visitor. Yet always was he disappointed—the burglary, as far as he could tell, was never repeated—and Minerva, tired of staying so close to the farm, began prodding for their course to stray farther and farther distant.

This did not go unnoticed by the demon inside Lyman. As much as he tried to keep it gagged, there came a day it finally seized Lyman's voice during their stroll. "I am very fond of the memory I have when you came to the stone house with a basket, and we picnicked some way in the woods."

"I am too," Minerva said.

"I'm glad. Yet something about it troubles me. Were your motives fully transparent, that afternoon? You can tell me if someone put you up to it. I won't be upset."

"What an odd question." She looked at him sidelong. "If you want me to confess that my desire for your company was greater than the want of a comfortable lunch at the Consulate, then I confess it freely. But to suggest I am a puppet to someone else's whims strikes me as a bit uncouth, Tom." Her pace increased so that she walked several steps ahead of him.

Deep inside himself, Lyman throttled the demon with white knuckles.

He caught up to her. "I'm sorry," he said very fast. "I've never told you this, but that day while I was out someone rummaged through the house. I suppose they were looking for money or silver."

"So you believe I was in league with a thief?" Her face, usually so disposed toward him, now contorted with some opposite feeling. "That I was to distract you?"

"Absolutely not." He stuttered and stammered. "What I'm trying to say—poorly, I realize—is that perhaps someone *suggested* the idea of a picnic lunch to you, and innocently—completely unknowingly—you took it as your own plan, and unwittingly abetted him."

Minerva said nothing for a long moment. "The plan was my own, and I told no one about it."

They walked in icicle silence.

"It may interest you to know," she said, "that Joan Alby told me she has seen some men lurking about the edges of the property. Further, at dusk a few nights ago, my mother said she saw a stranger near the Consulate. When he spotted her, he ducked into the trees across the road as if he didn't want to be seen. She told my father about it."

"I hadn't heard about this."

"Of course you hadn't. What women on the farm do you speak with besides me?"

Lyman made no parry to that blow. "What did your father say?"

"He said he would keep lookout for danger, but that jumping into ditches or behind trees is not a punishable offense in the state of Connecticut."

"I see." They continued, Lyman's mind spinning like clock gears. "Well, that explains much. I apologize, Minerva—a thousand times I apologize. You understand what I meant? I would never imply you would intentionally aid some villain."

She slowed to a stop and covered her face.

In that moment if Lyman could have stepped outside himself and laid his fist across his own jaw, he would have done it. "Minerva." He gently laid his fingers upon hers to pry them away.

She let them be pried. Her cheeks were flushed, her eyes damp. "Had anyone else said those words—they wouldn't have stung so sharply. They hurt because of what you mean to me."

Everything in Lyman's head, the suspicions and anxiety and the fresh terror that he had been found, suddenly collapsed like butter in a warm pan.

"Minerva." And suddenly his lips were on hers.

The full unabbreviated name of the place was the Bonaventure Farming Cooperative for Agricultural and Scientific Inquiry, although no one who hadn't visited would know that fact as the sign nailed beside the front door of the Consulate was the only medium wherein the whole title could be expressed. In conversation it was simply Bonaventure Farm or, curter still, Bonaventure.

The first word of the name, Lyman came to understand, resulted from a vote decided early in the farm's first days, a simple blessing of good luck upon the experiment. *Farming Cooperative* referred to its economic structure. It was the latter part of the farm's title that held the most importance for its founder, a fact that Lyman learned as he spent time with Grosvenor in the overgrown field behind the cabins.

"You have never asked me, Mr. Lyman, why we have christened the main house *the Consulate*," said Grosvenor to him as they dug, "but you must have guessed. It is because that was our first building when we began, and it is still where we first greet guests when they arrive at the farm. It is nothing less than our embassy to the rest of the world."

Lyman, with some reluctance, found himself conscripted into his apprenticeship of earth moving, which usually occurred after supper. There he would be, sitting at the table, chatting with Minerva, when suddenly her father would tear the napkin from his shirt collar and implore Lyman to join him in the field. There was no avoiding it, though at least Lyman avoided the clearing up after the meal, a chore the men were expected to conduct in balance to the women's preparation of it. Lyman would have very much liked to have avoided the digging as well, remaining tableside to laugh and talk with Minerva, or at least retire to his bed in the stone house unmolested.

"The Consulate is where we, the plenipotentiaries of the new regime, greet those citizens of the old. To them we must demonstrate that a lifespan can be expended at something better than mindless toil in a factory or a shop or on a wharf. Everyone must work to feed himself, it's true; yet they must also spare a few hours of the day to minimize the evils of this world through experimental progress."

As Lyman worked, Grosvenor would soliloquize on soil types and ratios of compost to sand or the corn varietal best suited to the Connecticut climate. It was not enough to grow food or for the farm to support itself financially, he informed Lyman: it had to contribute something original as well.

Lyman listened and nodded, often pausing to lean upon his instrument or wipe a handkerchief across his face.

"Nature wears many robes, Mr. Lyman, but we must tease the secrets out of her pockets. God has seen fit to give us the intellects to do so. In time, all that is mysterious to mankind will be unriddled."

"Including, I hope, the bones you're looking for." Lyman tried very hard to make it a joke, to keep the exasperation from his voice, yet in all of their hours of digging, they had failed to disinter so much as a mouse's toe.

"Patience, Tom!" said Grosvenor. "I keep Bonaventure's greatest discovery hidden in my office—that thing which we found here in this very field when we laid this foundation. When I finally show it to you, I need you to understand what it represents. Or, shall I say, what is at stake."

"And what is that?"

For a moment, Grosvenor said nothing, his face as impassive as granite. "Some things at Bonaventure," he said finally, "are not what they may appear to be. The knowledge of this, of this true state of things, is a heavy burden. I want someone who understands what needs to be done if Bonaventure is to prosper. As I said before, an apprentice of sorts."

Lyman nodded. "If you mean to say that Bonaventure is not on the steadiest financial footing, I regret to inform you it's no secret. As much as has already been hinted at, by you and several of the others."

Drapery fell across Grosvenor's face, a shadow of frustration and disappointment, and somehow, instinctually, Lyman knew he had said an inopportune thing. Yet why it was wrong or what he should have said in its place escaped him.

"Yes." Grosvenor set down the shovel in his hands. "In regard to that."

Every hair on Lyman's arms stood on end.

"I've been speaking to some of the other members of the community," said Grosvenor. "Some believe that a better qualified craftsman would have improved the stone house to a greater extent by now. They even suggest you may not be a carpenter at all."

Lyman could guess the fountainhead of this distrust. "Some, or just Mr. Sutton?"

But Grosvenor, to his credit, did not attempt to pretend the barn door was shut when the horses were so clearly in the pasture. "Please don't blame Mr. Sutton. He was a broker in his previous career, and like me, his training has made him particular about numbers and details. He only wants what's best for the farm."

"Which is why I find Mr. Sutton's preoccupation with past careers so curious. What does a broker know about sowing and reaping?"

"I believe Mr. Sutton's point is that, unlike him, you were explicitly recruited to Bonaventure for your skills."

"And I believe he has no right to complain. If I had not come to Bonaventure, the stone house would have remained a ruinous heap in the woods. Currently it is much more so."

"Perhaps. Or would it have been further along had someone else arrived in your place?" Grosvenor asked. "Bonaventure's dilemma is one of expansion. We need more hands to grow, but before that can happen, we need more beds for them to sleep in. That is why Mr. Sutton counsels selectiveness with whom we recruit at this stage."

"Yet isn't that against the very tenets of Bonaventure? Isn't the goal to cast the old customs into the waters and instead raise new fish at the ends of our poles? Your own daughter dreams of a day when there are no carpenters or farmers, when anyone regardless of sex or birth can perform any task or chore with equanimity."

Grosvenor chuckled. "I am Aristotle undermined by a sophist." He peered at Lyman through the lenses at the end of his nose. "Let me ask you pointedly: are you a carpenter, as you described in your letters to me?"

"What I am," said Lyman, drawing his spine straight, "is a subscriber to the Bonaventure project. I own a full share. I believe in Bonaventure—and if there are doubts about *that*, then as testament to my sincerity please refund my hundred dollars and I'll be on my way."

"You're serious?"

"If such a demonstration quiets those suspicions of yours or anyone else's, then yes."

Grosvenor fixed Lyman with frozen stillness. "Suspicion is a terrible emotion, I grant you. But often, it is not unwarranted. For example, I suspect a great many things about you, Mr. Lyman."

"Such as?"

"Such as your reticence to unhand your luggage that first day we met, as well as your payment of the subscription in full. You see, many of the others haven't paid the balances they owe—and yet you paid the whole fee on your very first day."

"Do you mean to tell me," said Lyman, "that the others aren't even fully paid shareholders?"

"I mean to tell you that I think you hold a great deal of money in your possession, which you have secreted somewhere at the stone house."

Suddenly two things became crystallized in Lyman's imagination. The first was that the digging exercise was, from the outset, a mere pretense for Grosvenor to arrange this moment. The second was that now Lyman knew who had rifled through his belongings during the picnic.

"Please don't worry yourself unreasonably," said Grosvenor. "I have no cares where the money originated. What I'm suggesting is that perhaps you and I are better," he searched for the words, "better *furnished* than the rest. And as such you are uniquely positioned to invest in Bonaventure to a greater degree."

"That's an interesting assessment," said Lyman. "Yet tell me something. I also recall when I subscribed that a regular dividend is due to all fully paid members. I remember it mentioned in our letters as well."

"Ah, well," said Grosvenor, "that's just a trifle—"

"How many of these dividends have you actually paid over Bonaventure's existence? I mean, I'd be willing to pay more if a large dividend could be *guaranteed*. But I'd expect more than a trifle."

The two men faced each other, and in the adamant set of Lyman's jaw, Grosvenor understood him; and in the anxious glance and quivering lip of Grosvenor, Lyman knew *him*. Neither was a carpenter nor the manager of a successful utopian venture. Both men were the perpetrators of very different fibs; each recognized his counterpart as a member of his own species, a brother of the same fraternal order.

Lyman pulled on the hem of his coat to straighten it. "David," he said, "I think we must come to an understanding."

"Yes, Tom," said the other man. "I agree that would be best."

Just as one cannot hope to pen a menagerie of zebras and giraffes on the shoulder of a road without expectation of passers-by to halt and stare at them, so too did Bonaventure attract its share of gawkers and gogglers. More often than not Lyman, sequestered in the woods with his stone house, remained ignorant of them; but every so often when he was working some chore at the Consulate or helping in the fields, he would glance up to see a party of well-dressed excursionists, usually attended by Grosvenor, watching him as they would a monkey peeling a banana. Newspapers spilled a great deal of ink on transcendentalism, most of it unkind, and for Saltonstall readers, a colony of adherents in their midst was too much a distraction to resist. Bonaventure was a circus that stayed put. While charging sightseers a nickel for a walk around the farm wasn't the most lucrative of side-businesses—nor was the penny for a cup of lemonade afterward—the overhead was small, so no one argued against the profit.

Besides, as Grosvenor would often point out, such was Bonaventure's mission.

Yet there are only so many times one can scratch his buttock or armpit, then turn to find a half-dozen witnesses to the event, or look up with an apple halfway to one's mouth to behold an audience leering outside the fence rail, before it agitates the nerves. Quicker than any magician's student, Lyman soon learned to vanish from the scene upon the approach of outsiders.

Not far from the Consulate lay a hillock shaded by clusters of white birches. From that vantage it was possible to observe the comings and goings of the strangers, and it was there that Lyman would escape to wait out any disturbance. He soon discovered he was by no means the first Columbus to plant his flag on that particular West Indies, for he was often joined by the young daughter of the Albys, who likewise shared his distaste at being subjected to voyeurism.

"My name is Judith Alby," she said upon their first encounter. "It's pleasant to meet you. Are you the replacement for Mr. Bradway?"

"I don't think so," said Lyman as he took his seat. "Who is Mr. Bradway?"

"He was an Englishman who stayed at the farm for a while but he left abruptly. A lot of people come and go here."

She sat cross-legged at the base of a birch. Lyman guessed her age to be around twelve years.

"People arrive here with all kinds of ideas," she continued, "though rarely do those ideas involve hard labor. The farm is like a canvas for them to paint upon but eventually when they don't like the picture, they leave."

Lyman was somewhat taken aback by this sermon delivered by so small a prophet. "What then is your idea for this place, Judy?"

"*Judith*. I have no ideas for it. Nothing grand, anyway. I came here because my parents did."

"So why did they come here?"

The girl plucked a grass blade and placed it in her mouth before answering. "It was my father's idea. My mother would join the Shakers if she could but my father is very much against it. You can imagine why. My mother's sort of Shaker in spirit, which is why I'm an only child, or at least will be until the spring when I shall have a baby brother or sister.

I suppose no woman is a fortress. It will be a sister, I hope. I would feel bad if it was a boy."

"Ah. You want a little playmate."

She looked at Lyman as if he was a dolt. "What good is it growing up a man *here?*" Her hand waved airily at the farm before them. "The only lesson taught at Bonaventure is how to sit around and dream. If a boy raised here ever left, he'd be in for a rude shock. He'd never be able to find work. He'd just wind up back here, or somewhere like here, or in some slum. This place is a land of lotus-eaters, at least for boys. My mother and the other women work as hard as they ever did on the outside."

Lyman took some offense at this slur against his sex. "Men just perform their work faster so they have greater leisure. It's a proven fact that men have stronger constitutions than women."

"Tell that to Mr. Hollin." When Lyman's expression communicated ignorance, she asked, "They haven't told you about Mr. Hollin?"

"No," said Lyman. "Was he another farm member who left abruptly?"

"In a manner of speaking," said the girl. "He was a young fellow, very idealistic and enthusiastic, one of the originals to join. Our first February here a bout of influenza tore through the farm. Everyone had it at some point. I should emphasize that included the women and me. Of all of us, Mr. Hollin was the only one who failed to recover."

Lyman shrugged. "A boy dying of sickness doesn't prove laziness on the part of the men."

"You haven't heard the story's end. Mr. Hollin was the first to die at the farm, so the question arose of where to bury him. Mr. Grosvenor chose a spot on the edge of the woods and made a service of it. A couple of days later Minerva went back to the gravesite to lay some flowers on it only to discover it had collapsed into the earth. A sinkhole—they had buried him atop a sinkhole. So Mr. Grosvenor organized the men, thinking to pull poor Mr. Hollin free to inter him somewhere more peaceful, only they couldn't find the body. They dug and dug until finally they gave it up for lost."

"What does that prove besides bad luck?"

Judith sagely regarded the farmstead. "It proves little, but it suggests intent. I think the men buried Mr. Hollin there because they knew the earth would fall in and they were too lazy to spade down the whole six feet. Mr. Grosvenor is quite fascinated with the geology of this place. He knew what he was doing."

Lyman's ears burned with incredulity. He stood and brushed off his trousers. "I must say you're a suspicious child, Judith. One wishes a little of Bonaventure's idealism would wear off on you."

In reply Judith lay back on the grass to stare at the bits of sunlight filtering down through the leaves. "Perhaps it will in time. I suppose I'm committed until the end."

If you know nothing about the geography of Connecticut, just know this: the soil there is terrible. The entire state is nothing but a pile of rocks both large and small, which for the most part have been covered with a layer of earth just thick enough to permit the growth of green things. Every inch of tillable space in Connecticut only achieved its status because some farmer and his sons painstakingly removed each cobble and stone from beneath the blade of their plow, thereby creating a narrow island of fertile field adrift in a rolling sea of stone and root. This meant that very little of the two-hundred acres of Bonaventure was developed into either field or structure, leaving the abundance as wild as when the Natives first trod their moccasins upon it.

Minerva, being her father's daughter, knew a thing or two about the land. The early colonists, she informed Lyman, had established their farms in the intervales, which was their name for the spans of fertile soil between spines of trap rock—called such after the Swedish word *trappa*, which meant *stairway*. In their daily walks Lyman and Minerva rarely pursued the same route twice, resulting in the continual discovery of some new prospect. During a given jaunt their path might lead between red maples and eastern hemlocks, the slopes rising gently to shelves of stone wet with moss or hanging ferns or trickles of water; the next it could open into a broad flatland of grass and pokeweed, the sun shining upon a wall of talus in the distance; and then the track might darken and narrow, ascending to a ridge where they'd shimmy through a tight notch in the trap rock, their shoulders brushing the sides. They waited out rain showers beneath overhangs and tentatively peered over the edges of cliffs. Manmade walls, their gray stones splattered by pale green lichen, crisscrossed the woods, and sometimes they would encounter a mossy stump, cleanly sawed through and the trunk crusted with conks of bracket fungus lying beside it, and they wondered aloud who built the walls and who cut the trees. They picked their way through quaggy lowlands and hand-in-hand bridged streams along the backs of fallen timber.

There was a particular day, a cool and clear afternoon where the leaves seemed like bright flakes of paint falling from Heaven's house, when the pair had just come around a bend in the path to catch sight of an odd woman standing on a gray humpback of rock not far inside the tree line. Though the weather was mild, the woman appeared to be wearing three overcoats with several layers of filthy shawl beneath, and the parts of her face that weren't buried beneath coils of gray hair were nearly dark as the stone. Because she had several sauce pots and pans lashed to a large pack on her shoulders, Lyman more properly heard her before he saw her. The woman clanged and banged with every twist as she danced upon the rock, scrutinizing the earth around her. When she finally glanced up to see them watching her, the woman said, "Watch'n your step—I ken there's a turtle about."

Minerva's face lit up like the dawn. "Bitty! Bitty Breadsticks!"

"Aye," said the woman, preoccupied with scanning the ground. She whirled in circles as if expecting an ambush from behind.

The pair approached her, careful not to toe stray terrapins. None were apparent. "I'm afraid I don't see any turtles," said Lyman. "Even if I should, they're never a terrible threat to people."

"Oh," said Bitty Breadsticks, "the turtles 'round here sure enough are. They're *snappers*, these ones. Ferocious diggers."

Minerva held in a laugh. "On my honor, Bitty, my friend Tom here has lived in the house nearby for several weeks now and he says he's yet to see any animal beyond a few birds in the branches, let alone a turtle."

"It's true," said Lyman.

Bitty looked at him sharply. "What house nearby? You mean the old *Garrick* house?"

"If you mean the stone house, yes."

"You haven't. The house's ruined."

"I've been repairing it."

"You been livin' there? *Sleepin'* there?"

"Yes." And then an idea occurred to Lyman. "Would you like to come see? We could make you supper, if you wish."

Bitty stared at him a moment longer and then—gingerly, on tiptoe—stepped off the rock and crossed over toward Minerva. "Let's haste away," she said low into her ear. "I don't like it when the turtles eavesdrop."

It had been Lyman's experience, elbow to elbow with the sailorly crusts of the Manhattan wharves, that beneath the thick rinds of graybeards and old salts lay the soft fruit of gossip if only one had the patience to spit out the seeds of nonsense that inevitably riddled it. Bitty, for all her antipathy toward Lyman and the stone house, could muster no dissent when Minerva showed her the contents of a small basket she had packed for a tea picnic in the woods. After finding an agreeable spot that the old vagrant pronounced free of turtles, the trio were soon enjoying an apple each while rashers sizzled in a pan over a cheery fire. Lyman did not hesitate to also produce a small bottle of Newport rum for supplementing their hot tea, offering it at the earliest opportunity so that Bitty's tongue wagged with the meal.

It had the intended effect. Lyman was relieved to learn, for example, that Bitty had indeed been the figure on the road to lunge into the trees upon being viewed by Mrs. Grosvenor. "Your mum don't like me much," Bitty said to Minerva.

"Yes, well," said Minerva, "more properly she does not care for your habit of hanging around the kitchen door for days on end, begging cups of coffee and table scraps." Then she added to Lyman, "Their last encounter ended with Bitty on the swat end of a broomstick."

Whatever Mrs. Grosvenor's feelings toward the itinerant old woman, her daughter Minerva didn't share them; in fact, Minerva possessed the foresight to appreciate Bitty for what she was—an eccentric in a world bursting its stitches with solicitors and bankers—rather than what she wasn't. Bitty traveled a circuit among the towns and farms between Lyme and New London, panhandling and rummaging through garbage and junk heaps for trade-worthy bric-a-brac. For the past week she had, unknown to most of their community, been sponging off the charity of Mrs. Alby over by the cabins, but with her patience finally extinguished, Bitty had been forced to head toward the next destination on her tour. She did not intend to linger in the area—particularly this close to the stone house.

"You needn't be so afraid of it," Lyman told her as they stared into the flames and digested. "I'll admit when I first heard the violin music my blood ran a little chilly too. But I've come to discover it's just a trick of acoustics."

"You rascal," said Minerva with surprise, "so you *have* heard the music."

Bitty growled deep in her throat. "The fiddlin' is Sed Garrick's doing."

"Sed Garrick? Was he the Garrick who came from England?"

"Aye. From Dunwich on the coast."

"The Garricks were the original settlers of the farm," said Minerva.

"I remember," said Lyman to Minerva. "Your father mentioned it my first day here. Something about the Garrick family exiled from England and the town sliding into the ocean." Then he said lightly to Bitty, "Does Sed Garrick still haunt the basement, playing his violin?"

"Don't mock me, young fella." Bitty squinted at him. "The fiddlin' isn't fiddlin' at all. It's *them*, tryin' to lure folks close."

The fire cracked and popped. The sun seemed to drop faster on the horizon. "And who might *them* be?"

Bitty glanced over her shoulders, much as she had done when the couple first encountered her. Yet instead of answering Lyman's question, she said, "It's Sed Garrick who's to blame. It's he who taught them that trick. He played fiddle himself, see. Before'n him, they hunted as anything hunts, with strength and speed. As an animal hunts. But it was Garrick who lectured them in cunnin.'"

"Whatever are we talking about?" Minerva asked.

Bitty's voice sank lower. "You reckon, that's what got him booted out a' England to begin with. What happened to Dunwich, if 'n you can imagine. Old Man Neptune took it for his own. And they over there, the townspeople and the elders, they understood what was causin' the tides to come rushin' in and the earth to dissolve under the soles a' their shoes. Oh, they may a' not known every bit, every chapter and verse—but they knew enough. The scratchin' beyond their cellar walls and the rumblin' under the streets and the holes openin' up and swallowin' stock and even folks themselves, if 'n they was foolish enough to wander far at the wrong times of day and night. And they kenned old Garrick had learned to discourse with those under, and told them where to go and when to eat in return for what they could bring him out a' the earth."

"I'm afraid I've lost the thread," said Minerva. "One moment we're talking about violins in the basement, and the next we're talking about someplace in England."

"Oh, aye," said Bitty, whose weaving followed its own warp and weft. "Dunwich it was—called Dommock in the old Anglo-Saxon, the capital of East Anglia where the bishops once held council and the Knights Templar kept their dark sentinel. A city a' churches, a' priories and chapels, that one by one fell into the sea. You think it was an accident, young fella? *Do you?*"

Lyman shrugged, his disregard for her shifting into embarrassment for himself.

"'Twas no coincidence that a place as holy and righteous as Dunwich eroded bit by bit into the sea," said Bitty, tongue and tone both scolding. "Dwindlin' and shrinkin' until nobody was left but those few who kept indoors or walked straight lines between thresholds. No, they knew, the townspeople and the elders. They knew somethin' lived among them. Beneath them. And they cottoned Garrick knew that fact better than any."

Minerva said, "I still don't understand. What *something?*"

Earlier Bitty and Lyman had passed the small rum bottle neighborly between them, with Minerva abstaining. Now Bitty held the empty bottle tightly in her grip, forgotten, and addressed Minerva in her roundabout way. "There's some'n believe Sed Garrick brought them over when he came. But I can't see how he'd a' managed that, and besides, the Indians had myths about them going way back. The Mohegan and the Pequot and the Narragansett, they may not've agreed on much but they agreed on the noises. Said it was a god, name a' Hobomoko, down there shaking the world, and their soothsayers and wise men would interpret the rumbles like a Gypsy reading chicken bones. *Matchitmoodus*, they called this region—the Place a' Bad Noises. The Puritans thought the Indians was Devil worshippers, though truth is, they was less about worshipping old Hobomoko and more about steering on his good side. And when they sat on his left hand, well, they gave Matchitmoodus wide berth."

The dusk closed around them like a fist. Lyman noticed how silent and still it was, as if the trees and rocks themselves leaned toward them, eager to hear the old woman talk.

"I can imagine some a' those stories reached Britain in letters and traveler's yarns and Garrick kenned the substance a' them. No, more'n like Garrick chose this place because they was *already* here, and if'n he could commune with them as was in England, he could commune with their American kin. He was already old when he came over, him and his family and his damned fiddle, and he lived longer still after settlin' here. Some'n say he was upwards a hundred and fifty when they finally buried him in the family cemetery, somewhere 'round, lost now. His age being a' result of the exchange he had with them, see. Carbuncles, they said—like ulcers or pearls they would give him from deep underground, to extend his years. They—"

At that instant, just as the crest of the sun's orb dipped beneath the unseen western hills and night decanted like syrup across the trees, a thunderclap broke the stillness and resonated under their feet. The Moodus Noises. The effect on Bitty was like paper in fire. Her eyes widened, her jaw dropped, the bottle fell to the leaves. The air trembled a moment longer, and then like a jackrabbit she was up. She snatched her pack with one hand and the frying pan with the other. "*If'n you run you can make the Whitney farm and the hayloft far off the ground*," she said aloud. Lyman sensed neither he nor Minerva was not the intended recipient of the words. To them Bitty said instead, "Get out a' these woods and somewhere safe, younguns. The turtles is on the move." Then she reached into her shawls, snapped something from around her neck, and pressed it into Minerva's hands. "You was ever kind to me, missy. Keep it close."

Lyman, while impressed by the show, remained uninfected by the woman's terror. "I told you before. A turtle is too small to do anybody much harm, Bitty—even a snapping turtle."

Bitty danced on the edge of the firelight. "You young fool, ain't you been listenin' to a thing I said?" She spread her arms like wings. "Them's Hobomokos is *big*."

And without another word she sprinted from the scene, faster than Lyman would've thought capable.

Minerva ignored Bitty's departure. Instead she knelt in the fire's dying glow, turning a small leather amulet over in her hands. Stamped in the brown hide was a six-petaled daisy wheel, the petals formed by the overlap of circles pressed into it. It reminded her of a sand dollar, washed up on the beach.

On any other evening, the brush strokes of Bitty Breadstick's fireside story, not to mention the color of her quick departure, might have been an artwork to inspire dread in Lyman. Instead he felt cool relief. Like the final scene of a play, all loose threads were tied in conclusive knots. The identity of the larcenist of Lyman's bureau drawers was indubitably Grosvenor, the old sneak; the strangers spotted hither and yon at Bonaventure were nothing more than a wandering madwoman. Or perhaps Bitty was responsible for both: Lyman suspected Bitty's fear of the stone house wasn't so sincere as to preclude the opportunity to nab an odd coin or loose coat button. Doubtless the Albys and Sutton and Presley and every inhabitant of the cabins would find small valuables missing when inventory was finally taken, long after Bitty had decamped for the Whitney farm.

I am safe, I am unknown—if there were emotions corresponding to those words, then they pulsed through Lyman's bloodstream.

In the woods, they stamped out the fire and Lyman returned a pensive Minerva to her father's house. It was by then suppertime, and after the meal and the chores, Lyman found himself returning to the stone house in almost utter blackness. Having come directly from their walk in the woods, he had neglected to bring a lantern for the return journey to his bed, and it always amazed him how dark the countryside became without the light. But he assured himself the distance wasn't far, and slowly and carefully set off in what he estimated was the correct direction. Before long the silhouette of stones blotted against the deep blue, and the latch of the front door was in hand as he stepped inside.

Fingers and thumbs locked around his throat.

Lyman gasped, clawing at the grip, and felt himself propelled backward. Once and then again and again lights exploded in the blackness as his skull was slammed into the stone wall. Then the hands vanished, and he collapsed on the floor, half-senseless.

There were sparks and then flames as someone started a fire in the main grate. Another figure took a taper around the room to lantern and lamp until the area was well lit. From his vantage on the floorboards, Lyman saw shoes pass before him, though he had no ability to count or determine how many pairs there were. His vision had attenuated almost to pinpricks; his ears rang.

Gradually he became aware he was being addressed, and he looked up.

One of them sat in a chair by the fire. The other lurked nearby, though where precisely Lyman couldn't say.

"Boy, we sure had a hard time finding you, Caleb," said the man in the chair.

Lyman's eyesight broadened slightly, and the ringing sank just a little.

"I have staked my reputation on finding men within sixty days of accepting the contract. Sixty days from handshake to apprehension."

Lyman tried to sit up against the wall. Failed.

"*Four months*," said the man. "The better part of four months, we've been tailing you. Isn't that right, Mr. Doyle?"

"I should know," said the other man, somewhere. "I've been there beside you, Mr. Myerson, every mile of the road."

"You certainly have, Mr. Doyle. Your diligence to duty is exemplary." For a moment there was only the sound of the fire crackling. Lyman smelled pipe smoke.

"Tracking you to Norwalk wasn't an issue, Caleb. The problem there, however, was what direction you had gone in. I made the mistake of thinking you might've gone to Ohio. I'm afraid much time was wasted in fruitless pursuit of that hypothesis."

"Poor Mr. Rose is still out there somewhere, pursuing that false trail," said the one named Doyle.

"Indeed," said Myerson. "But then we returned to the coffeehouse in Norwalk where you frittered away so many mornings. The proprietor kindly informed us that you spent a great number of hours there reading the newspapers. 'Well now,' we said to ourselves, 'maybe our good friend Mr. Caleb Kopf went somewhere he saw in the paper.' But how to find the newspapers you had been reading weeks prior?"

Myerson sucked on his pipe and pointed the stem at Lyman.

"It was wise Mr. Doyle who had the epiphany. The privy."

"I had it while *in* the privy," said Doyle. "Nothing like a strong cup of coffee to lubricate the bowels."

"Indeed. *In* the privy, *about* the privy. Because of course what does anybody do with an old newspaper? Why, they cut it up for repurpose in the privy."

The two men chuckled.

"So we took all of the paper out of the coffeehouse privy and we put them back together, and then we looked at the ones existent on those dates we knew you inhabited Norwalk. We learned those dates from your landlady, dear Mrs. Farrington. You remember Mrs. Farrington, don't you, Caleb? You stayed at her boarding house for a little over two weeks after steeple chasing out of New York."

"Very talkative is Mrs. Farrington."

"Oh, she's a garrulous woman, all right," said Myerson.

Lyman pushed himself up, spine against the stone. He managed to stay up.

"Well, one thing led to another and pretty soon we asked ourselves, 'Wouldn't it be something if old Caleb used part of that money he stole to buy himself a subscription to this socialist farm they're talking about in the newspaper?'"

"I confess I was very doubtful over such a theorem," said Doyle. "I apologize for my skepticism, Mr. Myerson."

"Nothing to apologize for, sir. We all make errors in judgment. I myself was the strongest proponent of Caleb's heading to Ohio. Before this contract, never in a million years would I have believed, with all that money in a carpet bag, that somebody like Caleb Kopf would go to ground performing manual labor so close to the city where he murdered his employer."

In a strange way, it felt good for it to be spoken out loud. The thing Lyman had been living with for so long, to be said and acknowledged.

"How did that feel just now when I knocked your head against the masonry? Must've felt much worse for Mr. Tallmadge."

Tallmadge. To hear that name from another's lips made Tallmadge real, made *the act* real. It had never been intentional. It had always been an accident, a set of circumstances—of reactions.

"Evil snowballs, don't it, Caleb? A few dollars embezzled to impress a young lady, and when Tallmadge confronted you—well, that's when the molasses hit the pie pan. Then you emptied the safe and ran. And for a while you thought you were secure. But here's the thing of it: Mrs. Tallmadge. She is *not* what I'd call the Christian forgiving type."

"More of the Book of Exodus kind," said Doyle, "vengeful and wrath-like."

It all started with an apple. Tom Lyman—or Caleb Kopf, as he was known then—had been in the warehouse when the men, careless with the block and tackle, swung a load too wide and tipped over a barrel. A dozen apples rolled nearly to Caleb's shoe tips. One of the stevedores righted the barrel and collected the loose contents but not before dropping one in each pocket of his coat; and then, conscious of Caleb's watching, tossed an apple underhanded to him. Caleb caught it without even thinking. Suddenly a flush of heat came over him as if he stood in the Tower of London with a ruby from Victoria's crown in his palm, and quickly he shoved it inside his coat. The stevedore winked at Caleb and returned to his lading.

Things went missing from the warehouse every day, Caleb knew, and not just apples. Commerce was measured in barrels and sacks and crates, never in individual units—what did it matter if a container held a hundred apples or only ninety-nine? Nobody ever counted the innards.

Nor for that matter did Mr. Tallmadge, Caleb's employer. That's what he paid his clerks for, to tally and sum and tell him, in a neatly written figure at the bottom of the right-most column, how many dollars and how many cents he owned. But in the days and weeks following the warehouse incident, Caleb came to reason that money was like apples: if too much was mislaid the absence would be noticed; but should just a few paper notes, here and there, vanish into a coat pocket, the omission was neglected.

Until it wasn't. One evening Tallmadge asked Caleb to stay late and then, once everyone else was gone, informed him that occasionally he audited his clerks' registers. There was a modicum of truth in what Tom Lyman had told Minerva: he'd courted a woman and sought to impress her with the misappropriations. Yet by that terrible sundown, the poor math in Caleb's book was too substantial to hide. Hot words were said, threats of arrest and lawsuits, and in a moment of panic Caleb grabbed the cast-iron door stop. He only swung it to shut up Tallmadge for a minute so Caleb could think, so he could straighten and make sense of his own story. It worked, in part—Tallmadge never uttered another syllable.

Myerson rose from the chair. He knocked the ash from his pipe into the fire, placed the pipe in a coat pocket. "She wants you to face justice, Caleb, though she has no druthers on whether it's a lawman or judge or anyone else who dispenses it. To that end, Mrs. Tallmadge has engaged Mr. Doyle and I to be the instruments of her will." He stood over him. "But first."

He grabbed Lyman under the jaw and hoisted him to his feet. Lyman hammered at the man's arm but Myerson ignored it, like a father discrediting the strikes of a bawling child.

"Where's the *money*, Caleb? We've searched the house—twice. Once while you were picnicking with your whore girlfriend, and another just now."

Myerson's fist smashed into Lyman's diaphragm.

"Where?"

He punched again.

"I'm afraid if you don't share it with us, we're going to have to *hurt* you."

The grip released and as Lyman fell, Myerson hooked a haymaker into his eye socket. Lyman spun to the floor.

Had they not laid another finger on him after that initial hello inside the door, Lyman would have gladly told them the location of the bag. He cared for beatings even less than he cared for rolling off roofs and whacking his thumbs with hammers; and he calculated the quicker he told them, the sooner the ordeal would end. But as it was, dazed and blurry-eyed and his brain sore and jostled in its case, at that moment he no longer had any recollection of the site. Where *had* he put the money?

Myerson picked him off the floor again, jabbed him in the chin. Lyman's head bounced off the wall behind him. "Where, Caleb?"

He was sure he would recall, if only it would stop and he could *think* a minute.

One-two in the ribs as he keeled downward. A third to the ear. "Where?"

Wait—what was this about anyway? Lyman forgot more and more.

Myerson knelt beside him and for variety's sake socked him with his left fist. "Where?"

He didn't know what they wanted. Only what he wanted. He wanted for it to stop. He wanted to see Minerva, one last time. To explain it to her.

Myerson loomed over him, his breath stinking and hot. "Where, Caleb?"

"*The basement.*"

Myerson looked up at Doyle. "What did he say?"

Doyle's eyebrows knitted together. He'd heard the whispered words distinctly, though Lyman's lips, split and drooling, had barely trembled. "It sounded like he said it's in the basement."

Myerson let go of Lyman's collar. They had already searched down there, found nothing. "He must've buried it."

The bounty man stood. "Bring him," Myerson said to Doyle. Whatever partnership and compatriotism had been in his earlier tone vanished; he spoke as an employer dictates to a wage worker. "I'll grab the lamps."

Doyle pulled Lyman's arm across his back, and by measures dragged, wrestled, and grappled him down the stairs into the dirt-floored basement. Myerson held a lamp in either hand, wicks high.

"Where?" He snarled at Lyman. "Goddamn it, I weary of this. Show me where you put it."

Lyman's head rolled on his shoulders.

"Hey," said Doyle, gesturing. "Look at that over there."

Myerson raised a lamp. He walked over and ducked his head beneath the stairs.

"Did you notice this before?"

"No," said Doyle. "Isn't that the damnedest?" The closer they approached, the more obvious it seemed: there was a corridor under the stairs that led somewhere else. "Like when the curtains rise at the theater, only with shadows instead."

"It's a passage," said Myerson. He stepped within.

Doyle wrenched Lyman to his feet and in moments the three arrived in the dome chamber. Doyle, tired of lugging Lyman's weight, dropped him on the edge of the cistern.

Myerson squatted, lowering a lamp inside the well. "What do we have here?" Setting down the lamps, he reeled in the line hanging from the top rung of the ladder. At the end swung a fish full of money.

The pair of men smiled and whooped.

"This'll buy a few sips of whiskey at the hotel tonight," said Doyle.

"Oh, and a big steak dinner too," said Myerson. "We'll be sure to toast you, Caleb."

They turned toward Lyman. During their brief celebration, he'd managed to crawl a few steps toward the passage.

"Now," said Myerson, "about that justice Mrs. Tallmadge so stringently insisted upon."

Doyle reached behind and drew a long knife from its belt scabbard. "I'll be quick about it."

"Think of your coat, Mr. Doyle." The bonhomie had returned to Myerson's tone. "You know from experience how wildly the blood spurts from an opened jugular. Yet here we have a grave already prepared." He waved toward the cistern and the metal grate. "All Caleb needs to do is hop in, and we'll do him the favor of closing the casket after."

"Aw," said Doyle, "I'm exhausted from carrying him. You throw him in."

"No need. Caleb will deposit himself, won't you, boy?"

Myerson walked around so he stood between Lyman and the passage. He drew his foot back, then swiftly kicked him. Lyman reeled backwards.

"That's it, Caleb! Direct yourself toward your coffin."

Lyman rolled onto all fours, tried to crawl anywhere but.

This time Doyle kicked him.

Then Myerson. Then Doyle again, until Lyman lay on the edge of the cistern, his arms crossed over his gashed and bleeding face.

"No more," said Myerson. "No more cotillions on your semblance, Caleb. You go on now and climb down that ladder so we can lock you up snug."

Lyman lay there.

"Either you do it—or we do it for you."

Arms wobbling, Lyman pushed himself to his knees. One of his eyes was swollen shut. Blood streamed from his broken nose, splattering on the dirt. His breath rasped.

"Go on, boy." Myerson and Doyle stood beside him, toes on the rim.

Lyman reached down for the top rung of the ladder.

"Go on."

If Lyman had any thoughts at that moment, they barely rose above the most instinctual, the most base. In the cistern, at least, he would be away from them. Reduced to an animal level of pure sensation, Lyman was only aware of pain and the impulse to escape its source.

Yet as his head hung over the precipice of the cistern, staring with a single working orb into the darkness where the lamplight failed, he became aware of another feeling, another sensation. He'd encountered it before, on that very first night in the stone house. The whiskers of his beard bent and twisted from the air blowing upon them, and he intuited, deep down in the bestial awareness of his consciousness, that something very large sped toward him at very great speed.

With his remaining strength, Lyman shoved himself away from the cistern.

An enormous white mass rose straight from the opening, lifting up and above them as it filled the entire width, and clamped its jaws around Myerson's head. For an instant it hung there, a marble pillar, talons tight against its bulk, tiny eyelids sealed shut, and then gravity seized it. It dropped out of sight, pulling Myerson with it.

Neither of the remaining men moved or uttered or blinked. Then a horrible sound echoed from the cistern, a ripping and rending, and two things happened in quick succession. Doyle screamed. Lyman lashed out with his foot, kicking the back of Doyle's knee. Doyle's leg folded, his body twisted, and he plummeted over the edge of the well, his transit mapped by the continuing howl. Then another sound issued from the cistern, as of a thick branch being snapped in a giant's hands. The scream immediately ceased.

Lyman flipped over, injected with new stamina, and crawled on elbows and knees toward the passage and the stairs and the woods and any spot on the globe except that basement.

"No one should go."

An inarticulate cry scrabbled from Lyman's throat. He crawled.

"No one should go. I shall give thee what thou most craves."

He reached the wall and turned, expecting it to be right behind him. But he only saw the mouth of the cistern, and the grate in the dirt, and the bag of money, and the two burning lamps.

"What," Lyman said. It was everything he could summon. "What do you want?"

For a long moment, the only reply was the sounds of tearing and chewing inside the well.

"To be. Our good friend."

Lyman shook his head. "No."

"You want. A. Good friend."

"I have friends."

"Mr. Doyle, Mr. Myerson." Something popped and crunched.

"Not those two. They weren't my friends. I mean real friends."

"Real friends? You want a good friend."

"I'm leaving. I can make friends in a new place."

"No one should go. I shall give thee what thou most craves—a good friend."

"You're just saying that so you can eat me," said Lyman, "when you're done with them."

Pause. *"Absolutely not."*

"And how am I supposed to believe you?"

"What an odd question."

Lyman wiped his sleeve across his mouth, staining it. If the thing had wanted to devour him, it had not lacked for opportunity in the preceding weeks.

"We are brothers and sisters?"

"Not until I know what you want in return."

Chomps and cracks and mastication.

"Why didn't you grab me the first time I came down here? Or any other time for that matter. Like you did with them."

"You were the right man for the job."

"How? What job?"

"Patience, Tom!"

Lyman shuddered. "I am bargaining with the Devil, it seems."

"Yes, as a matter of fact."

"What then is the price of my soul?"

For a long moment, Lyman's invisible conversation partner made no reply and the room grew so quiet that Lyman wondered if he was alone. But just as Lyman parted his lips to repeat the question, a whisper echoed from the cistern, the sighing voice rustling through the air like a breeze through falling leaves.

"A comfortable lunch."

CHAPTER TWO

Minerva Grosvenor closed the thin volume and held it in her lap for a long time. Her impressions rambled and raced in a kind of downhill confusion, dominated perhaps by a kind of elation, the feeling of having searched under every dresser and bedstead for some misplaced thing like an earring or a letter, only to finally discover it in the last place she looked. What she'd found inside the volume—more of a chapbook, really: saddle-stitched and very light—was the key to a lock that everyone at Bonaventure acknowledged to exist but none knew how to penetrate.

The book was titled *The Prose Romances of Edgar A. Poe*. It had been published the previous year and contained two stories. The second story Minerva did not care for, nor did she quite understand the author's intent in writing it; but upon reaching the back cover, she immediately turned to the beginning to read the first again. This story, after a long and winding introduction, involved the solving of a seeming impossibility: a situation in which two women, a daughter and mother, were graphically murdered—one stuffed up a chimney! the other's head left hanging by a strip of skin!—inside a room where all the doors and windows were locked, and yet where no trace of the killer could be identified. Nonetheless the narrator's friend, Dupin, pinpointed the culprit, using only the powers of faculty and observation.

Her thoughts after this second reading, originally unsettled, tumbled like grapes or blueberries through sieves pocked with decreasingly smaller holes, sorting by circumference, collecting by kinship. Everything, Minerva realized now, was a mystery, an unanswered question.

Take Bonaventure itself. The commercial: the farming, the crop yields, and varying prices of the produce brought to market. The metaphysical: the community, with the disparate wants and intentions of its members. Each was a question that had yet to be asked. But this man Dupin, this character of Poe's, could string together questions and make a reply to each. Every silent answer led to the next question like Theseus's ball of twine through the labyrinth, until finally he could respond to the unspoken thought in his friend's head, having followed alongside ever since the narrator was jostled by a grocer blocks ago. For Dupin, that ability—that gift—was nothing *more* than a source of amusement, a broom to sweep away the dust of boredom. What waste! To Minerva it was nothing *less* than the pinnacle of the mind, a synthesis of ratiocination and intuition. It was the very goal of Bonaventure's experiment, wrapped in a gruesome tale of blood and horror.

When Minerva visited her father in his office to inform him it was now her life's mission to assist humanity in answering these greater mysteries—how shall we live? how shall we worship?—by reconciling the unanswered riddles of the everyday, he barely acknowledged her. He sat at his desk, a set of scales before him. One pan held a number of small brass weights stamped with the numbers of their ounces. The other pan had been hastily covered by a handkerchief just before Minerva's entry into the office.

David Grosvenor listened to his daughter's epiphany, though Minerva couldn't dismiss the almost tangible feeling that, having interrupted him, he was impatient for her to be gone. Eventually he nodded, and without looking up from the balance scales he suggested she offer her deductive assistance to Mr. Sutton, who had misplaced one of his hogs.

"And while you're at it," said Grosvenor, "see if you can't locate your friend Mr. Lyman. No one's seen him in nearly a week."

Mr. Sutton was adamant his hog had not run off. It was stolen.

"It so happened I looked out my window that morning and saw them rooting through the corn. I told Presley to pull on his drawers and yelled for Mr. Alby to come help. When we herded them back into the pen and counted, we realized we'd caught all of them save John Tyler."

Minerva knew, from some of the debates at the supper table, that Mr. Sutton was no booster of their sitting president, whom Sutton likened to a piece of livestock too stupid to understand what lay in store for it.

"Why do you think it—I mean the pig—didn't run off? From what you say, the gate had been open all night."

"The gate had been *opened* at night, more correctly," said Sutton. "Swine can't work a gate and there's no chance I or anyone else would have left the gate open after the evening slop for the simple reason that each of us knows how difficult it is to catch a loose pig. It's a chore nobody wants. I ask you, why would John Tyler mosey off to some far horizon while every other pig headed straight to the cornfield? No. Somebody came and took that hog, and freed the others to cover the absence."

A thief then, Minerva thought. Yet she couldn't imagine anyone leading a full-grown pig far on a rope leash. It began to dawn on Minerva that determining a course of events was difficult without a trail of gore and a bloody shaving razor.

"Whom do you suspect then? I hate to accuse anyone without more definitive proof, though even I must admit Mr. Whitney over at his farm is a very taciturn man." She could think of no other potential rustlers beyond the greybeard Whitney, who in the past had accused the Bonaventurists of misconduct after several of his prize milk cows went missing.

Sutton took a deep breath and appraised Minerva much as one does when he realizes his jacket is hooked on a briar and he stops to study how best to liberate it without tearing the fabric. "I have a man's name in mind but I fear you'll not care to hear it."

"Please do not think to shield me from cruel truths because of my sex. I think better of you than that, Mr. Sutton."

"That isn't why I hesitate." Sutton pursed his lips. "I am supposed to deliver the hogs to the butcher next week. John Tyler was the biggest of the bunch—three-hundred pounds market weight by my estimate. That's thirty pounds of ham at nine cents a pound; eighteen pounds of sausage at eight cents a pound; sixteen pounds of bacon at close to ten cents a pound; twenty-three pounds of chops, another six of ribs, twenty-eight pounds of roasts, all at eight cents per pound; plus ten pounds of stew bones and another sixteen pounds of fat-back at middling prices. That's near one-hundred fifty pounds of cuts totaling forty dollars, or nearly half of what each of us at Bonaventure, excluding yourself and your parents naturally, is supposed to have paid to become shareholders of the farm."

Minerva crossed her arms over her chest.

"I have always admired your intelligence, Minerva. I —"

"Oh please stop flattering me," she said, "and arrive at your point."

Sutton cleared his throat. "It's just—it has been intimated by your father that our enterprise is not as financially successful as we had hoped. At his suggestion, I assumed responsibility over the care and raising of the hogs because they're crucial to our survival. The loss of that forty dollars may, in the final summation, decide whether we are still here this time next fall."

"Are you suggesting someone might intentionally want to ruin us?"

"Not intentionally, perhaps. But I can tell you from personal experience that Bonaventure attracts its share of eccentrics. It may also attract worse." He turned his gaze toward the road leading to the far side of the property.

There was no answer when Minerva knocked on the front door of the stone house, just as there had been none when she had rapped a week earlier. The note was still pinned to the wood, though now its corners were curled, warning the reader that the occupant within was ill with fever, and that visitors were best advised to observe his self-imposed quarantine. That first time a week ago, alarmed that Lyman had not kept their usual rendezvous for their forest walk, Minerva had called through the door, hoping Lyman would hear, and when there was only silence, she returned daily with a basket of food left on the threshold. The empty basket that awaited her the next day suggested the patient was on the mend. And yet no one had laid eyes on the man during that time. How lonely and awful it must be, Minerva thought, to lay in one's bed, sweat-soaked and delirious, a half-mile from any assistance, all for the sake of selflessly protecting others from infection.

Out of habit Minerva tried the latch, expecting it to be locked. It always was. But to her surprise the door creaked open.

"Tom?"

She stepped into the house, waving a hand in front of her face to dispel the musty air. Immediately she crossed to the closest window and raised the sash, letting the coolness spill inside. "Tom? It's Minerva."

Nothing. She wondered if he was even at home.

"Tom?"

"The basement."

"The basement?" Minerva had no notion why he would be down there. "Where are you?" Perhaps he had fallen or was hurt; his voice sounded weak, barely rising above a husky whisper. She wandered toward the kitchen, opening the few doors she found and discovering only shallow closets, until she undid the bolt and found herself staring down a stairway into gloom.

She couldn't see him. "Tom? Are you there?"

"The basement."

A breeze blew upon her cheeks, warmer than the air outside. Carefully, not wanting to misstep and tumble into the unknown, she set the toes of her right foot upon the top stair.

Something gripped her arm, hauling her back. The door slammed inches from her nose and a hand threw home the bar.

His face was a melted candle of purple, black, and yellow, one eye swollen into a squint, his lips bloated like grubs beneath the coppery beard. Minerva shoved a knuckle into her mouth to stifle a scream.

"I know," said Lyman, "I've seen myself in the glass. It's better than it was, believe me."

"Tom—*what?* You said you were in the basement—" Her head tilted toward the door, but her eyes remained locked on him, unable to look away.

"No, no. You misheard. I was saying, *My face is on the mend.* I didn't want you to be shocked by my appearance."

For half a moment Minerva said nothing, unsure. Then she reached up to softly brush his cheek. "No fever could do this. You look as if you've been beaten."

Lyman pulled away. "I hadn't the courage to tell you. I—I fell off the roof."

"You've fallen before."

"Yes, but this time I broke my fall by landing on a rock. I was so embarrassed; I didn't have the heart to come up to the house and admit it to all of you."

"Oh, Tom." Impulsively she grabbed him, thrust her head against his chest. "I've been so anxious." After a moment she stood, wiping wetness from the corners of her eyes. "I'm relieved to hear you're not actually sick. Still, you must stop going on roofs."

"Yes, well, I think I almost have the hole over the summer kitchen fixed."

Minerva pushed at the pleats of her dress with her palms, resolute and yet unsure. "That's part of why I came. Other than my concern for your health, of course."

Lyman regarded her.

"Tom, I think you should know that *some* people at the farm— not many, mind you—but *some* people are worried that perhaps you aren't holding your own. That is, by not contributing enough to the community."

"I see."

"They suggest that you should have completed the restoration of the stone house by now. They even suggest you might be a poor carpenter, or perhaps have never been a carpenter at all. You mustn't think I believe this. I'm just repeating what's been said to me. They said that because everyone pays an equal amount to join, and through his or her labor each is allowed an equal share of—"

"But I haven't paid the same as everyone else," said Lyman. "I've paid more."

Her thoughts came to a halt. "What do you mean?"

"Didn't your father tell you? Quite recently I decided that I like the stone house so much I don't want to leave it. Your father said it was quite out of the question, that it was required to be the men's dormitory. We struck a bargain in which I offered him another twenty dollars a month for the privilege of living here in the house. Alone. I still have only one share in Bonaventure, of course. I only wanted more control over my living arrangements."

Minerva's eyes and mouth opened like flowers. "You're paying *rent?* But—why would Father allow that? It's against the very nature of Bonaventure, the egalitarianism of what we strive for. No one should be allowed to buy special favors just because they're wealthy."

"Minerva, please—is wanting to be in this house so desirable? Out here, on the opposite edge of the farm, away from everyone. It's not right to maroon a group in the wilderness and let them fend for themselves. Better for me to stay out here and leave the others to the comfort of the main house."

"That's not the point."

"Well, your father agreed with me." Or at least, thought Lyman, he agreed to the twenty dollar note. "But if the other members think I've been shirking work, I would be happy to help with the farming." The thinnest thread of indifference laced his tone.

Minerva cast around her, a little jumbled and lost. "You could assist Mr. Sutton. One of his hogs has disappeared."

"Is that so?"

"I don't presume you know anything about it."

Lyman spread open his palms. "Now where would I hide a hog?"
Minerva smiled a small smile. "Mr. Sutton is a very suspicious sort."
For half a moment, each was silent.

"It's not buying a favor. I would never think to do such a wrong."
Minerva nodded. "Perhaps there's some reason in what you say."
Suddenly she clasped him again. "I do hope you're well enough to go
walking with me again. I so enjoy our rambles."

Lyman hugged her to him. "I do too," he said. "It's good for me
to get out of this house." And although she could not see it, his gaze
lingered on the basement door.

When they next met to resume their woodland walks, Minerva was
much surprised at Lyman's appearance: though still a little puffy and
swollen and colored in the dustiest shades of plum, Lyman's face had
collapsed into something very like its old assemblage. Amazingly this
transformation had occurred over scarce days.

"I have been taking medicine recommended by a friend," Lyman
offered when pressed.

"What friend?" Minerva asked, perhaps too sharply. "A friend at
Bonaventure?"

"No. A friend down—*south*. My friend advised that certain
minerals when mixed with water would help reduce the swelling."

"Really? What minerals, exactly?"

Lyman let out a low whistle. "I'm afraid I'm not at liberty to speak
of it. It's a secret, you see. The recipe is a home remedy that my friend
tells me has been passed down for generations among his, ah—" Lyman
trailed off, finally returning to his thought to add the word, "family."

"Well," said Minerva, "I dare say this friend of yours down south
must live in Florida and possess the surname *de Leon*. He should
become a cosmetician and mix his minerals into ladies' toilette soap.
When applied to a body less injured, I expect they would restore whole
decades."

The pair had selected a gray overcast afternoon to restart their walks together, the air unusually warm but the breeze cool as it rained orange leaves upon them.

"You say the friend recommended your prescription, through the post I assume. It's odd that I don't see you up at the Consulate to request your mail," said Minerva after some moments' rumination. "Nor do I recall mail addressed to you ever arriving at the house."

Lyman shrugged. "I correspond rarely and when I do, I prefer to meet the postman myself to assure delivery and receipt."

"Do you worry about someone reading your mail?"

"Not at all. I worry about misplacement."

Minerva said, "So you lack trust in your compatriots."

"Mistrust and an acceptance that accidents occur are two very different emotions. Take Mr. Sutton's pig, for example. You've told me he insists it was stolen. Yet there's no evidence the hog's disappearance is anything more than an accident."

"It's odd that a hog that size has not reappeared, though. Father sent word around to the other farms and nobody has seen it."

"This corner of the state is hardly New York or Boston. A hog could live the remainder of its lifetime in this wilderness outside human awareness."

"Mr. Sutton is certainly upset about the hog's loss, however. Accident or intentional, the result is the same. An evil has been done."

One of the great mysteries of Bonaventure, Lyman had discovered during his time there, was that while its members agreed upon a course of newfound communal living both for personal reward and as an example to the rest of the planet, they certainly disagreed on the precise shape and form of that idealized existence. Modeling the men and women of tomorrow demanded countless questions be asked today.

Take the merely practical, for example. If clothes betrayed wealth and rank in the greater world, should the farm members perhaps dress identically in simple smocks? If gout was the malady of kings and plutocrats, should their diets abstain from meat? These simple day-to-day unknowns invariably led to more heady queries. Should the members restrict their attentions to themselves or strive toward effecting change in the greater world? How could their experiment be regarded successful if in their self-concern they ignored the plight of the bonded slave or the diseased orphan? And so on flowed the questions to Lyman's eternal boredom, the uncertainties of the utopians ascending ever higher in great spirals until finally the wax of their wings melted and they fell one by one into an unanswerable Aegean.

When these discussions erupted, Lyman was always careful to refrain from comment or, if invited to speak, to offer the briefest of opinions. Yet it was common during their walks, after having shared farm gossip and commented upon the weather, for their discussions to likewise range into hypothesizing and intellectualism. Minerva never hesitated to speak her mind in a crowd; but the intimacy of the forest and their companionship encouraged Lyman to be less laconic in matters philosophical.

"I believe," he said, "it's an error to judge an action good or evil without knowing the purpose behind it. Rather the intentions of the actors are what should be scrutinized and weighed."

"So if a letter of yours was misplaced—completely without malice—by someone at Bonaventure, you would not begrudge the guilty party?"

"How could I?"

"But we have not discussed the content of the letter," said Minerva. "What if the letter contained information regarding an imminent invasion, addressed to the authorities? Or some other news that, if delayed, would cause harm."

"Then I would say the carelessness of the one who misplaced the letter is to blame."

"Even though he had no intent to do evil? And yet evil resulted nonetheless." She waved her hand. "It wasn't so long ago that such a thing was imaginable, the entire coastline of the state burned and ravaged by soldiers in crimson."

The routes for Lyman and Minerva's walks being rarely twice repeated, they had, while they talked, entered a new part of the forest. The path dipped between blocks of trap rock, the leaves barely carpeting the cobbles winding between them. The trees, many of them by this time stripped of their robes and shawls, perched atop the walls like naked crones.

Lyman replied with slowness as if considering each word. "The fault of the invasion lies with the invaders."

"That's beside the point. We're confining our interest to the mishandler. We suppose that if the letter had reached the authorities, the invasion would have been prevented. He had no intent to do evil and yet evil occurred nonetheless."

"Carelessness could be considered an evil."

"But that's not possible. No one *intends* to be careless with the post."

It was not for nothing that Lyman preferred tight lips; these roads led only to rhetorical snares and logical bear traps. "Then he committed no evil," Lyman said firmly. "Whatever occurred afterward is the fault of others. They're the ones with evil intent, not him."

Minerva was silent a moment. "I find that poor reasoning, Mr. Lyman."

"And how would you reason it, Miss Grosvenor?" He tried to keep the cold out of his voice, to pretend it didn't bother him. "I assume you value the result instead."

"No," she said. "I believe evil has nothing to do with either intent or result. Evil is merely the absence of good. The mishandling of your letter, for example, cannot be considered good, therefore it is evil."

Lyman considered. "What then is the source of good? In your worldview."

"Simply the desire to do good consciously in regard to every action, no matter how small. To do anything else is," she searched for the correct word, "careless."

The pair slowed to a stop; their path, if not their walk, had concluded. The thin canopy overhead opened onto slate clouds, mirroring a barren rock field below. Slabs zigzagged from the forest floor as if punched from the earth by a subterranean fist, its sterile loneliness further pocked by boulders and the odd tuft of grass. On all sides the field lay surrounded by black branches and red leaves, like Beefeaters standing at attention around some significant ruin, an almost perfect circle of erratic crag and stone sequestered among the trees. The isolation of it underscored the lifelessness of their strolls, the complete lack of squirrel or doe or fox, and Minerva imagined the far side of the moon could not be half as forsaken as this spot.

They mutually decided to turn back rather than risk a twisted ankle, so the day at least ended on an agreeable note.

During Lyman's absence from the farm's activities the sweet corn had been collected; but now remained the work of husking it. The corn meal returned from the miller would serve as the basis for much of the farm's comestibles over the winter months, while the proceeds from the corn sold at market would be folded into Bonaventure to purchase the things they could not themselves produce—which were many.

After breakfast on the chosen day, every resident gathered in the yard beside the Consulate, took his or her seat, and went to work on the mountains of green corn dumped on the ground. If a mound shrank too greatly, then some of the men would visit the corn crib, returning with full barrows to replenish the stock. The husked corn was tossed into a wagon bed for eventual return to the crib, and quickly a side sport developed of fancy tosses and over-the-shoulder hooks, rewarded with cheers or catcalls depending on the athlete's aplomb.

It was a long and tedious chore. Fortunately, to make the time pass faster Grosvenor had engaged the services of a schoolteacher from New London to present a lecture while the Bonaventurists worked. This wasn't unique; Lyman was told that visits by lecturers and scholars was a common occurrence in the bleak weeks of January snow and February ice, and likewise Grosvenor or some of the others were occasionally invited to share their views at lyceums and parlors in the neighboring burghs. The theme of the teacher's talk—whose name was either Hoyt or Howson or maybe Hewlitt, no one could say exactly afterwards which—made it obvious why he had been chosen, dovetailing as it did with Grosvenor's personal sensibilities.

He spoke on the inherent conservatism of society. "How often it is, friends," he said, "that we keep old customs close to our bosoms for no other reason than they have long lodged there. Like letters from some youthful lover who has since married and moved elsewhere, we maintain these customs yellowed and careworn in our breast pockets, representative of something that was meaningful to us once and yet has no modern purpose today."

"Much like our useless attachment to clothes," said Mr. Presley.

"Yes! I mean—what? *No*. It's not the same at all," said Hoyson, "but regardless these customs and conventions lie all around us, so much so that we ignore them until we are blind to their presence. As an example, look here! Since I have arrived at your fair farm, I have noticed *these*."

He strode over to the side of the Consulate and, kneeling, parted the long grass to point at symbols carved into the foundation blocks of the house. The symbols were round, like wheels, with segments of other circles carved off-center within so that the overlapping ovals created a petal effect, sometimes five petals, sometimes six.

Lyman, who had never seen the carvings before, looked quickly at Minerva. She sat absorbed, her husking forgotten.

"These are called daisy wheels," said the man. "They are wards intended to keep evil at bay. They were very popular in previous centuries in rural England, where the superstitious farmers would carve them into foundations or beams and lintels to keep devilish spirits out of their houses. The idea was that evil would become lost in the marks' twists and turns like a walker in a maze, and thus couldn't penetrate beyond. Doubtless these marks were carved by the original settlers of this farm."

"I had thought they were sand dollars," said Minerva, "carved as some reminder of a day at the beach."

"Indeed! I see how you could believe that. The resemblance is similar. Nevertheless," said the man, rising to his feet, "they are nothing quite as lovely. Instead they serve as reminders of how ignorant and irrational our forefathers could be. And yet by clinging to these outdated beliefs, we are little different from those who would burn old ladies at the stake because of a lazy eye or a mole on the cheek."

Everyone soon settled into the drudgery of the work and the

droning of the lecturer faded into the noises of tearing husks and twisting stems. Eventually the lecturer's throat ran dry and he vanished into the kitchen for a cup of tea. Meantime the others joked and teased and made contests of their husking; and when that failed to amuse, they sang songs. Lyman knew few of the words.

One thing broke the repetitiveness of the day. Minerva had noted that of all their company, there was only a single absence: that of Mr. Sutton. The vacancy was made the stranger by Mr. Presley's admission that he'd not laid eyes on his cabin mate since late the previous afternoon.

Then, during lunch, Grosvenor came hurrying around the corner of the house with a letter in hand. He announced it had been tacked to the front door and was addressed to the members of Bonaventure. Everyone left off their meal and crowded around Grosvenor while he read it to the company.

It was, as supposed, from Sutton himself, and amounted to an apology and explanation of sorts in which Mr. Sutton announced that he found the labor of the farm too much for his constitution and had decided to retreat to his brokering in New York. He further added that the shame of his weakness prevented him from saying his good-byes in person, and therefore he had skulked away under cover of night. There was no use chasing after him on the road or writing to him in the city, Sutton insisted; his mind was resolute, and he wished nothing more than to put his adventure at Bonaventure forever behind him.

There was a great murmuring at this as everyone agreed this action was most unlike Mr. Sutton's character, for while he could sometimes make himself boorish on the subject of abolitionism, all concurred it was the very same fiber and tenacity that had made him a leading figure at the farm. Several of the ladies wept into their napkins, upset at their friend's departure without a face-to-face *adieu*. Grosvenor did not know what to make of it, shocked by the erraticism of a man he considered steady as stone, and after concluding his oratory, he sat humbled in his seat, refusing to touch his coffee.

Minerva herself found her mood weighted by leaden ballast. Only days before she had discussed with Sutton the vanished John Tyler and been impressed by his devotion to Bonaventure's future.

The feeling persisted throughout the day, distracting her thoughts as she performed her chores rotely. Sutton's departure was both odd and yet completely understandable; so contrary to his manner and yet logical in light of his view of the farm's tenuousness. Here was a new enigma, then: what would Dupin think? Come late afternoon, as she stood in the kitchen with the other women preparing supper, Minerva happened to glance out the window to see the menfolk retiring from the husking, the denuded corn returned to the crib. On an impulse she threw down her paring knife and headed toward the cabins.

Mr. Presley—having just returned home and still fully clothed—was unsure how to react to Minerva's presence in his cabin; she was, in fact, the first female to ever cross its threshold. She *prowled*, in his estimation, about the single room, scrutinizing and studying; picking up a redware mug and setting it back down, or fingering through the shirts left on their hooks over Sutton's bedstead. Truthfully Minerva did not know what to search for either. Meantime Presley watched her, not knowing whether to sit or stand or what to do with his hands.

In addition to his clothes, Sutton had also left several bundles of letters tied with string in the drawer of the cabin's desk. Minerva hesitated a moment whether to examine them, but then realized they were fair game by reason of their abandonment.

"It is a favorite pastime of Mr. Sutton's," said Presley, "or *was* I should say, to write and read letters at day's end. I prefer to read educational and uplifting books, myself."

"I see the letters are bundled by sender," said Minerva. There were more than a dozen packets.

"Yes. He kept a voluminous correspondence, though I don't know all of the recipients entirely. I know he has a sister in Pennsylvania toward whom he feels great attachment. Also a good friend he worked with at the Exchange Board in New York."

The letters, of course, consisted exclusively of missives sent *to* Sutton. Minerva pushed around the drawer for a diary or unsent epistle but found no sample of the man's writing, no clue or explanation beyond what her father had read aloud at lunch.

Presley stroked his beard. "As a matter of fact, Mr. Sutton had received a letter in the post just yesterday, from his friend in New York—I saw the return address clearly. We had quit our labors. He sat to read it over a cup of coffee before dinner when suddenly he leapt up in some agitation. Then he grabbed his coat and stormed out the door, the letter in hand. I assumed it was bad news, and he had gone for a walk to cool his head. That's the last I saw of him."

Early on a breezy Wednesday in October, the members of Bonaventure pulled the wagon out of the barn, hitched Bessie the ox to the tongue, and piled as many as they could into the box. David Grosvenor climbed into the seat, his wife alongside him. He tapped Bessie's shoulders with the lightest brush of the whip and slowly the wagon started down the road to Saltonstall, its cargo laughing and chattering too loud. Meanwhile a bunch of the men, Lyman included, released the mature hogs from their pen. Under Mr. Presley's direction—the swines' master, Mr. Sutton, having abdicated his position to his lieutenant—the men formed a phalanx around the hogs and, goading them along with switches, followed the wagon to town. It was the day of the Saltonstall Agricultural Show.

It was a merry parade, the women facing backwards with their legs dangling off the open tail board, pointing and advising as the men and pigs followed them like the children of Hamelin. The hogs required constant attention, as very often one or another would attempt to penetrate the cordon walling them in while others, exhausted from what was doubtless the most strenuous exercise of their lives, would occasionally decide to halt and lay down in the middle of the road. Fifteen minutes into it, Lyman thought it was the most arduous walk of his life, and thirty minutes into it he decided it was also the most absurd.

Once, when the pigs had picked their pace to arrive close to the wagon, Minerva leaned over the rail and wiggled her fingers at Lyman striding next to the spoked wheel. "Kiss my hand!" The women beside her tittered.

"I daren't," he said, "not with your father and mother riding up front."

"If you're too prudish to give me a kiss, I'll steal it from you." Minerva grasped the rail and pivoted over the side, pecking Lyman on the cheek. The girls cheered, the men howled, and for their part Mr. and Mrs. Grosvenor pretended deaf and dumbness. Lyman's ears burned.

The show had erected a large canvas tent in a field just beyond the town center, with a number of smaller tents and gypsy carts orbiting it. The utopians disembarked from their wagon and the pigs, sensing the excitement and hurrying faster, were corralled into a waiting pen. Their labors for the most part complete, the Bonaventurists dispersed to their own amusements.

Lyman and Minerva immediately found each other and headed for the main tent, cramming onto the rough plank benches inside to watch the many acts. Not all were equal to the others. There were several contests wherein blue ribbons were dispensed to the fattest hog or finest ear of corn. Lyman was just about to excuse himself to go buy a bag of roasted chestnuts when boys appeared rolling giant orange pumpkins like boulders before them, and even Lyman's cynicism was abated when they began weighing them. More exciting still was a plowing competition in which a number of men lined up at one end of the tent behind their plows and nags, and at the blow of a horn raced down the length, leaving deep furrows in their wakes. Minerva clapped and cheered while Lyman wondered who would repair the field once the show departed.

After the contests, the crowd spilled out into the little avenues formed by the carts and stalls where a gray and chilly afternoon had descended. Straw had been thrown onto the churned mud, lit by lamps and tall smoking tapers. Minerva snuggled close to Lyman, the air damp without the sun.

"Here is our perfect city," said Minerva. "Boulevards of grass under rooftops of boughs. No vermin, no beggars. See how easy it is to achieve? The only question is why we don't pull down our cities of stone and brick tomorrow."

"Ah," said Lyman, "but this neighborhood is ephemeral. It isn't made to stand more than two days. Should all our cities be so?"

"I see no need of cities lasting for more than two sunrises. The buildings and taverns would come together, trade would be conducted, and then the whole would dissolve into mist. What business is so consuming that it requires more time than that?"

"The council to decide what to call each town would alone last a week."

Minerva suddenly pointed. Just ahead, a tent, smaller than the main, had been staked into the grass. A sign over its flaps read *Menagerie.*

Immediately she pulled Lyman in its direction, breathless in her demands that he pay the penny admission. "Do you think they have an Ourang-Outang?"

Alas, while the proprietor—a girthful man with a mustache of eccentric length—did allow a small tailed monkey to climb onto Minerva's shoulders, the zoological demonstration failed to contain anything larger than a house cat. Lyman strode among the tables, peering into the cages, not terribly impressed to learn such a wide and diverse array of rodents and weasels populated the planet.

"A proud look, a lying tongue."

Lyman, by this time, was accustomed to hearing eerie voices uttering strange truths over his shoulder, yet nonetheless it never failed to unnerve him. He froze as if dipped in Rosendale cement; his skin turned icy; his stomach contracted into a knot, reducing his breath to short, shallow puffs. He had yet to hear the voice outside the stone house—or, at least, very far outside the house—but now it had, to all audile appearances, followed him to town.

Slowly he turned toward the speaker.

"A proud look, a lying tongue, and hands that shed innocent blood."

A gray bird regarded him from its perch upon a wooden stand, head cocked. A fine bracelet was cuffed around its ankle, connected to the dowel by a long chain knitted from tiny links. *"These six things doth the Lord hate,"* it said, and slowly it closed the lid over its shiny black eye in a wink.

"Ha, ha," said the proprietor, coming over to the stand. He stuck out two fingers and the bird obediently stepped onto them. "Merlin says such witty things, don't you boy?" He held the bird toward Lyman for closer perusal. "A grey parrot from the jungles of Africa, sir. One of the few of God's creations capable of human speech."

"Better than most," said Merlin.

"Remarkable," said Lyman, still shaken. "I thought only we humans possessed the faculty to form our thoughts into words."

"Strictly speaking, that's true, sir. Birds like Merlin can only mimic words and phrases they've heard before. They don't voice original ideas. His original owner, for example, was fond of the Book of Proverbs, and therefore so is Merlin. Still, I have always been impressed by how well he knows *when* to repeat certain words. He is an uncanny judge of character and timing. Aren't you, Merlin?"

"Better than most."

Minerva had come up behind Lyman and stood on tiptoe in open-mouthed wonder at the bird. Lyman's blood beat harder, very aware of her hands wrapped around his waist and her breasts pressed against his back. "My goodness," she said, "your pet Merlin is a better conversationalist than most Methodists."

"Ha, ha. No doubt, miss. Though I'm afraid were you to have tea with Merlin, the discourse would grow cold sooner than your cup. His vocabulary is very limited."

"How many words does he know?" asked Lyman.

"Oh —" The proprietor thought. "I would say no more than a hundred words. Again, they are only words he has heard spoken before." The proprietor dropped his voice. "I always insist that no blasphemies be declared near him. I have heard other parrots say the most shocking things."

"Doth the Lord hate," said Merlin.

"Such beautiful tail feathers. Bright red," said Minerva. "And just look at his wicked talons." She stroked his foot with a forefinger. Though the curve of his beak remained unchanged, Merlin seemed to smile. "The scales of his legs are almost reptilian."

"Indeed, miss. I have often thought likewise. Frequently has it made me wonder about the true nature of the relationship between the lowest serpents in their holes and the birds in the branches overhead. The Maker's design is truly mysterious."

Merlin cocked his head at Lyman. *"A lying tongue,"* he said, *"better than most."*

There is never a lack of chores to perform on a farm, and more than one plowman will opinionate that tasks multiply rather than lessen once the crops have been collected and the calendar descends into its penultimate month. With the harvest complete, the hogs sold, and the corn shucked, Bonaventure turned its focus toward winter.

Repairs number among such tasks, and a particular antemeridian found Minerva and her father along a back acre mending a fence broken by time and weather. These were the chores Minerva liked best, the ones that took her outside the Consulate and, more specifically, outside its kitchen. Shelling peas and kneading dough were necessities she understood well, but they were jobs best left to rainy days. When the sun shone and one's spine and arms were strong, what finer way could there be than to spend the hours out-of-doors, notching posts, and fitting rails? Not to mention more satisfying. Peas and bread rarely last until the morrow but a solid fence will sustain years.

As they worked, Minerva scanned the tree line and was reminded of John Tyler the hog, who she imagined somewhere beyond—either wild in the woods, or more likely, butchered on the plate by some thief. This thread of thought led her to other disappearances as well.

"I cannot help but take Mr. Sutton's departure personally," she said as they dug to extricate a broken post from its hole. "He isn't the first to leave without an *auf wiedersehen*."

Her father stepped upon his shovel, driving it deeper into the soil at the base of the post. "I think his note explains all. He was driven by humiliation and leaving so quickly saved him embarrassment."

"Still, the hurt remains."

"For you, perhaps, and the rest. I believe too often it's ourselves we wish to save from hurt, and in so doing, we cause incidental hurt to others."

"Do you remember John Bradway?"

"I do." Some emotion clouded her father's face.

"He likewise left without a farewell."

"The circumstances of his departure were much different."

Minerva ceased at the digging. "Why? Did you see him leave?"

"Indeed. I was the last to see him go because I was the one to dismiss him."

"Father," she said, "you didn't."

His daughter regarded him with such intensity that Grosvenor was forced to stop and lean on his shovel. "I'm sorry, Minerva. I know you had tender feelings for each other. But I learned things about his past, things you don't know, and I felt he did not have your best interests in mind."

"What sorts of things?"

"Things I will not repeat. Things that don't matter now. Regardless, when I confronted him and asked if they were true, he admitted they were. I therefore asked him to pack and depart the farm immediately."

"And that is why he never said good-bye to me," said Minerva. "Did anyone else see him go?"

Grosvenor shrugged. "I don't recall. He left within the hour of our conversation."

They worked for another few moments in silence.

"I know you remember Clemmie Russell," said Minerva.

"Of course." Grosvenor smiled. "She was a sweet girl."

Minerva eyed him carefully. "And presumably still *is*. What was the context of her leaving, again? I fail to recollect the details."

"Her mother had taken ill. Clemmie had received a letter in the day's post and departed by nightfall."

"Yes. That's it. Again, I never saw her off. Strange that she's never written to us since, if even to let us know her mother's condition."

"Out of sight, out of mind, so the saying goes. Probably Clemmie forgot all about us in the turmoil of caring for her mother." Grosvenor smiled at her. "You're a suspicious sort this morning. What's bothering you?"

"Why, nothing at all."

Minerva laid aside her shovel, and pulling together, they dragged the post stump from its bed. Then they carried a fresh post from the cart and, with some huffing and puffing, placed it in the hole. They paused to catch their breaths.

"Minerva," said Grosvenor, "you must understand the differences here at Bonaventure." He cleaned his glasses on his handkerchief. "We strive for egalitarianism, it's true. But in the end, it doesn't exist."

"How is that?"

"Because it's my name on the deed." He replaced the glasses on his nose. "I speak plainly with you because as my daughter you bear some of the risk. Subscribers—people, *friends*—may come and go to Bonaventure, and take it and leave it as they wish. And that is precisely what they do, in the end. They come for a while, as it suits them, and then depart, again, as it suits them."

"There are the subscriptions, however. It's not as simple as rolling a mattress into a bindle and wandering off down the road."

"No, you're right—and thank Providence for that. If it weren't for those stakes in Bonaventure, the turnover would be even higher. Yet even such money is no firm tether. Mr. Bradway asked for his money back, which I returned immediately. Mr. Sutton will probably do so once the full flush of his embarrassment passes. As I recall, Clemmie Russell never paid that much to begin with, so little was lost there." He looked hard and frank at her. "If Bonaventure fails, then the members lose only what they've paid. They can always return to their old lives or start over again somewhere new. But if it fails, we—you and I and your mother—will be bankrupted. We will be indebted and hounded by creditors, forced into penury. In a word: ruined. We have much more to lose than the any of the rest. So much more. That's why I wouldn't worry yourself over departures. Let them go. We're the ones who can't leave."

Minerva nodded and bit her lip, the gravity of her father's words falling on her like a shadow. And yet they still didn't quite explain an absence of simple good-byes.

✦ ✦ ✦

The following morning, as she descended the staircase, Minerva saw the young man before he saw her.

He sat on the bench by the front parlor window, his arm on the ledge, the other idly fingering the planter's hat in his lap. As he gazed through the glass his head was turned slightly from her, and with her mind's scissors, Minerva couldn't help but cut the sharply defined features of his silhouette from black card stock. She was sure he was unaware of her presence, and yet the way he sat seemed almost a pose, as if he was an artist's model silently listening to the pen or the brush as it moved over a canvas. For whom the pose was intended Minerva couldn't guess, unless it was something learned after a lifetime of being self-conscious about his own handsomeness until it finally became *un*self-conscious.

Not willing to be caught staring, Minerva intentionally brought her foot down on a specific lower step. At the stair's squeak, the man sprang to his feet.

"Beg your pardon, miss," said the man, "I didn't see you there." His face was scrupulously clean shaven.

"Another new recruit! No need for *begging* or *pardons* at Bonaventure." She held out her hand. "I'm Minerva Grosvenor. So glad you're ready to join our undertaking."

Instead of shaking her hand, however, he pressed it to his lips before releasing it. "I have to beg your pardon again, Miss Grosvenor. I'm not here to join your commune."

"Oh?"

"I have some business with your father, David—I presume he's your father?"

"Yes, that's right." He did not strike Minerva as a banker or businessman; his clothes were too simple, his sleeves and hems too worn from travel. "And you are?"

"My name's Isaac Rose. I introduced myself to one of the other ladies of the house and she let me in. She said your father had gone for a walk but would return soon and I should wait."

"I see. I apologize for the mistake."

"No apology necessary, miss. I'm actually glad his absence provides an opportunity to wait. I am in awe of the view outside your window." He gestured with his hat toward his former perch. "I've been told that nothing is finer than New England in the autumn, and I'd yet to behold it until these last few days."

"I'm afraid you're a few weeks past our best foliage." Minerva detected a slight drawl in his voice. "Have you traveled from the south?"

"I *am* from the south originally, miss—northern Georgia, in fact. But I've most recently come east from Ohio, where I was traveling for work."

"That's a fair distance to travel. I hope your trip was a success."

"It was not, I'm afraid to say. But I believe I may find more fruitful results here in Connecticut."

"And what is your profession?"

Rose hesitated before answering, smiling a bashful smile. "I find people who are missing. Long-lost relatives, folks who may have inherited wealth. Folks who have something coming to them."

Involuntarily, Minerva stepped closer to him. "Like a ratiocinator?"

Rose looked at her, then smiled again. "I'm afraid I don't know what that word means."

"I apologize. It means, *an investigator*. Someone who investigates a mysterious event or circumstance—like, say, a crime—and determines the truth of it."

"Well, I don't investigate crimes so much, although I'm sorry to say that too often the circumstances of the people I seek involve a crime of some sort."

"Really."

"I'll admit something to you, Miss Grosvenor, although it does no credit to my reputation." That smile again. "Currently I am in need of my own services. I have a pair of business partners, a Mr. Myerson and a Mr. Doyle. Do you know them, by any chance?"

"I can't say I'm acquainted with either gentleman, no."

Rose frowned. "It's strange. They left a letter for me in a coffeehouse in Norwalk indicating I could find them here in Saltonstall. Unfortunately, no one in the area seems to have met or seen them."

"Being somewhat removed, we don't make it into town very often, so I can't speak to their whereabouts. I must say, however," Minerva said, "I believe we have very much in common. I'd like to help you in any way I can."

"I'm much obliged to you for that, Miss Grosvenor."

Minerva shook her head. "You mentioned you were from Georgia. It's funny, but just now I remember a gentleman here at Bonaventure once commented that he had a southern friend who corresponded with him. You wouldn't know Tom Lyman, would you?"

"Now it's my turn to say I'm unacquainted with someone. Looks like we both need to broaden our horizons and meet more people."

"Perhaps I could introduce you to him before you go?"

At that moment, the front door opened and Minerva's father walked in, fresh from his morning ramble.

"I'm pleased to meet you, Mr. Rose," said Grosvenor after introductions were made. "I'd shake your hand but I'm afraid I need to wash them." Minerva noticed her father's hands were chalky with stone dust, as if he had been digging or breaking rocks.

"Mr. Grosvenor," said Rose, his palm extended and his tone very sincere, "no man should ever be ashamed for the soil of our blessed country that covers his hands. Both my grandpappies were farmers, as is my pappy to this day. To have hands dirtied in pursuit of a man's honest profession is an honor, never something to apologize for."

Grosvenor beamed ear to ear. "Well said! Bonaventure would be privileged if we had more men like you." And they clasped hands firmly.

When they finally disengaged, Grosvenor waved toward his office. "Why don't we sit down and discuss how I can assist you, Mr. Rose."

"Thank you," said the young man. He nodded toward Minerva. "It was the greatest pleasure meeting you, Miss Grosvenor."

"Oh, by all means please call me Minerva."

"You flatter me. I'll be sure to ask after your Mr. Lyman before I depart. Maybe we do have friends in common after all."

Then with another nod, the pair stepped into the office and her father shut the door behind them.

Being an inveterate walker, Minerva often took strolls regardless of Lyman's schedule, or anyone else's for that matter. Sometimes Judith the young daughter of the Albys joined her on these woodland rambles. Each found they could confide in the other because their circles rarely intersected: one lived in the Consulate, the other in the cabins; one was the daughter of the founder, the other the daughter of subscribers; one worked in the kitchen and the other in the fields, when not learning her Rs. It's easier to speak freely with someone you don't know too well.

Such is the bottomless energy of youth that Judith rarely walked a straight line; instead she would often parallel Minerva on the trail, weaving around trees and stumps or hopping from rock to rock. That day their conversation wandered as much as they did, jumping subject to subject from the farm's chickens to Judith's schoolwork to her pregnant mother to a suspected romance between Nancy and Abraham, two of the farm's members. Finally, the dialogue alighted on the topic of John Tyler the hog, and whatever had become of him. Judith was an unshakable proponent of the thin-air hypothesis.

"Do they ever bother you, the stories about the farm?" Judith asked.

"Which stories? You mean the ones about people vanishing?"

"Yes. Bitty Breadsticks told me about them once. But not too much because I think she didn't want to frighten me."

"I doubt anything can frighten you. No," said Minerva, "I can't say they particularly do. They're just ghost stories handed down over the generations, becoming more dramatic over time. I suspect the Garrick family wasn't popular around here and the stories were intended to disparage them. Like the witch trials of Salem. Someone didn't like the Garricks, so they spun lies about them being witches to hurt them."

"I think people really did vanish. They probably fell into sinkholes like the one that swallowed Mr. Hollin's body."

Minerva frowned. The final resting place of Mr. Hollin, somewhere so deep below the ground as to be unseen, had never rested easy with her. More should've been done even if she didn't know what that *more* was. "If sinkholes were the case, then people would just say so. They would say, 'Watch out! The old Garrick farm is full of holes!' The stories would maintain the rational explanation. Instead they veer into the irrational, which is a good clue they're not trustworthy."

Judith's expression grew thoughtful. "So you're saying people prefer the fiction. You like reading fictions."

It was impossible without a looking glass to see if she blushed, yet Minerva certainly felt her cheeks grow hot. As Mrs. Alby often sent Judith to the Consulate to collect their mail, the girl knew about Minerva's habit of ordering novelettes through the post. Minerva tried hard to keep this secret from the rest of Bonaventure: fiction, being a falsehood of sorts, was therefore antipodal to truth. Her tastes, of course, did not run to the pornographic, which was the common perception of such slim volumes; but the infamy of the lowest often clings to the reputation of the highest, even when respected names like Poe decorated their covers.

"I'm saying there's no non-fiction to prefer. I doubt anyone ever disappeared here in the first place. The case of Mr. Hollin aside, there's no holes into which anyone could fall."

"What about the cave?"

"What cave?"

"The one near the stream. I often see your father there, talking to himself."

Minerva stopped to look at her. "Show me."

It was less a cave than a crevice between two adjoining slices of rock, set into the slope above the water's edge where the stream ran dark and slow. According to Judith, on more than one occasion she had spied the elder Grosvenor there.

"He'll sit and speak into it as if it was a megaphone," said the girl, "and then listen to the echoes as they come back. But the echoes are wrong."

"What do you mean, wrong?"

"Sometimes they say words your father didn't originally say."

Minerva crossed her arms, suddenly cold. "Such as?"

Judith shrugged. "I've never been able to hear clearly. I never wanted to get that close. They were just whispers, really, but I could tell sometimes the words came back different. Like one time your father talked about salmon swimming upstream and the echo said something about returning to the sea. It's a good trick."

Minerva regarded the crevice with misgiving. "Only a child smaller than you could fall in there," said Minerva finally. "My father is fond of geology. I'm sure it's some acoustic anomaly he's discovered, that's all."

"Maybe they're not echoes," said Judith with slyness. "Maybe he's talking to Mr. Hollin. Hey!" Her face brightened. "We should tell people *that* whenever we're in town. We'll start a new story about the farm—a new fiction—all by ourselves."

But the older woman didn't hear. Minerva stood rigid and motionless as if listening to some distant sound, yet when Judith likewise paused to listen, all she heard was graveyard silence.

"Judith," said Minerva very quietly, "we must go back."

"What's wrong?"

Minerva shook her head, scanning the trees around them. "I just have a feeling." She held out her hand for Judith's. "Hurry."

They began their return, walking at first, then speeding into a trot, as Minerva held onto the girl with one hand while the other hiked her own skirts above the knees to free her legs. Judith had to jog beside her, lashed to a runaway horse she couldn't control. Every third step became a leap to keep up with the taller woman's stride.

Then with a rumble the ground under the trail collapsed and Minerva pushed Judith away as she spilled downwards into a suddenly yawning pit, clawing wildly for purchase, pebbles and stones raining upon her. A thick root soared past. Minerva grabbed it, her whole body jerking to a halt.

For a moment she dangled as sand drizzled past. Above her, Judith peered over the rim, her face white and wide-eyed. "Minerva," she said, "Climb. *Climb.*"

Gasping, Minerva planted her heels into the pit's side and hand over hand, pulled herself up the root. Judith's mouth opened and closed but little sound came out.

She reached the top of the root. A gap of several feet still existed. "Judith—please."

But Judith just stared beyond her. From the bottom, if there was a bottom, emerged an awful, improbable sound.

"Suspicion is a terrible emotion."

"Judith. Your hand."

The girl shook her head, not so much denying Minerva as denying what she beheld beneath her.

"Please."

Judith thrust out her arm.

Taking one hand off the root, Minerva began to fall again. She lunged for Judith.

Judith caught her. Her strength wasn't enough to pull her up but Minerva used her arm as she had the root, stamping her boots into the loose earth and pulling her way up and over the edge.

Together they scrambled away from the pit into the leaf litter, hoarse and tearful. They looked back toward the pit. It lay silent. When she dared to peek over its edge, all Minerva saw was an empty depression with nothing but sand and rocks at the bottom.

Our thoughts in the nighttime are not like those during the day. Having fallen asleep in a world that flows by logic, by cause and effect, by customs and manners and etiquette—a world defined by predictability—we awake after our first sleep in a confusion of looming shadow and creaking floorboard. With few others awake, there is no reliance on sociability for our cues; we cannot look to them to inform us. The light of reason is subsumed by whim and mercury, leaving us with our senses as lonely guides through strange forests. We stare: what is that shape at the end of the bed? Then we remember it's only our clothing thrown over the back of an old chair. Our force of will becomes the singular hand that molds the clay back into its daylight form, and yet as soon as we turn our attention away the shape springs immediately back into lumpen mystery.

Minerva lay in her bed, the hour of the night unknown to her. The day had passed in a confused jumble. Upon their return to the Consulate, the story of the sinkhole had been met with a flurry of alarm—the roaring collapse had been heard in the fields but dismissed as the Moodus Noises. Brandy was produced and given to Minerva in brief sips; meanwhile Mrs. Alby had bundled Judith off to their cabin, saying the girl was babbling and feverish. Minerva thought Judith quite cogent. The issue lay in the inability of the others to comprehend what she said.

The brandy made Minerva sleepy and after being helped to bed by her mother, she had tumbled into dreamless depths the minute she touched the pillow; and yet from there, some indeterminable time later, she had risen to wide wakefulness, buoyed to the surface by a single image in her head. It did not, as might be expected, concern the day's events.

It was the remembrance of Mr. Sutton's letter.

There were many strange things about it, not least of which was Sutton's anonymous and detached exit. So strong was his abolitionism that he had spoken at times, with at least some small degree of seriousness, of journeying south to free the slaves at gunpoint; and it was difficult to reconcile this firebrand nature with the image of a man skulking off in the early morning hours after pinning a letter to the Consulate's front door. And as both Minerva and Mr. Presley could testify, Sutton failed to depart with most of his belongings. That afternoon in the cabin Presley had muttered something about his friend's property being too crude for a broker's office in New York— it was no loss to leave it behind. Neither spoke aloud their suspicion that Sutton might at least have taken those items known to have some intimate stake with him, if only the letters from his sister.

If Mr. Sutton had fallen into a sinkhole, why would he have left a note?

It was always a joke at the farm, the supposed vanishings, made comical by time and the lack of connective tissue between the Bonaventurists and the original family. Before today no one, certainly not Minerva, ever stopped to assume the stories were true. Of course, for decades the farm sat empty, and the legend of it carried some weight with the locals. But not with the modern tenants.

And yet, lying in the dark, it suddenly did not seem so inconceivable to Minerva. Perhaps the Garricks *did* drop through soil one by one until none were left, save for the last poor fellow who fled west.

Sutton vanished as his hog John Tyler had vanished. As did John Bradway. And Clemmie Russell.

Minerva's thoughts between sleeps eddied and spiraled. In the center of her mind's ocean, a single berg of ice loomed larger than the rest, the others winding about it in slow orbits. They came together, jostled, rebounded, and flung themselves away in new patterns, and yet always gravitated toward the larger mass.

It was common in the evenings, after dinner but before everyone retreated to their slumbers, to hold some entertainment in the Consulate parlor or out of doors on the lawn. There would be readings of essays, either homegrown or from *The Dial*, or speeches or plays; the previous year Minerva had portrayed Hermia in Bonaventure's episodic production of *A Midsummer Night's Dream*, spread across four sequential nights.

Upon a recent night there had been a poetry reading, with the Shelleys and Byrons among the community rising to stand before the audience and, with sometimes quivering hands and trembling voices, share their own efforts. Mr. Presley versed his way through doggerel celebrating the life-giving benefits of the sun, while Mrs. Alby offered a few lines calling for the equality of women before the law. Yet no one had been more delighted than Minerva when little Judith Alby stepped before the room and announced, "On Obligation."

"We drive and beat across the frontier, taming the untamed land," she read, "yet traveling not so far as to leave behind obligation to our fellow man."

In a steady tone, her sheets of paper clutched before her, Judith praised the improvement of the American countryside and the innovation of its people, of its farmers and settlers, all the while reminding her listeners that such progress was worthless without responsibility to others. For these reasons and more, she intoned, the names Meriwether Lewis and William Clark should be held in higher esteem than Washington or Jefferson; and Minerva thought Judith made several clever couplings with seemingly unrhymable phrases like *Corps of Discovery* and *Sacagawea*. And while one metaphor regarding the digging of shallow holes seemed overused and, odder still, was accompanied by sharp glances at Minerva's father, who simply nodded and smiled in encouragement, throughout her poem Judith praised the loyalty among those early explorers of the wilderness, equating the tenacity of their mission to their fidelity toward each other.

"Friendship, like duty, is hard won but easy to lose—and equally it was shared by the men and woman in their hide-bound canoes."

The seats in the parlor were loosely arranged in two groups. That evening Minerva had chosen not to sit beside Lyman, or perhaps Lyman had chosen not to sit beside her; tongues bounced enough regarding them and their walks together, and Minerva did not always care to indulge the gossip of the butter churn or the hay bale. Yet rarely was he far from her mind. Greedy for a quick smile or a wink of affection, she turned to sneak a glimpse at him seated across the aisle.

How to describe what she saw, or her astonishment at the sight? Supportiveness, amusement, boredom; any would have been expected emotions. Instead she saw a man perched rather than sitting; a man whose hands gripped, not held, the spindles of the chair in front of him; a man whose spine leaned forward like a willow bent toward the water. Rivulets coursed down his cheeks and his nose sniffled. His eyes—his eyes adored. Minerva, far from taking a cursory peek at him instead stared openly, safe in her place far outside his attention. She doubted whether Lyman was aware of her or the others at all, or even the room or the house or the planet. For him in that moment, all that existed was Judith and her message of devotion.

How little we know each other, Minerva thought. One meets a person and paints a portrait of him using colors to our preference, and then upon confrontation with evidence outside their shared experience, the paint smears and bleeds. We assume people only exist within our eyesight; that they were born seconds before we met and die moments after we leave them. What an illusion it is to imagine that by spending a few idle moments in common company we comprehend another person. Not more than an arm span from Minerva was a stranger, a being moved by an emotion unknown to her. Something between love and uneasiness gripped her deep within. What tenderness lay beneath the bark of a man, Minerva wondered, that a child's poem could bring him to tears? Or should she rather ask what sin had he committed, what trespass against a brother had he effected, that could kindle inside his soul a remorse so intense that it flowed like warm mineral waters down his face?

Suspicion is a terrible emotion.

It was useless to lie abed, Minerva knew: sleep would never come, at least this night, until she received explanations. She rose and dressed quickly, throwing an extra shawl around her shoulders against the chill. When she was ready, she reached for the unlit lantern on her nightstand. Her hand hesitated. Instead she plucked up Bitty's amulet lying beside it, feeling its embossed arcs and circles in the thick leather under her thumb. In the dark it somehow seemed brighter than any lamp. Rather than tie it around her neck, she stuffed into the pocket of her jacket.

Any other time it would've been easy enough to creep downstairs and slip out the door without interference, but on this particular midnight, the front parlor was occupied by Mr. Isaac Rose. After conducting whatever unspoken business he'd had with Minerva's father, Rose joined Bonaventure for their communal supper and then—after gamely helping the other men in the washing up—was given pillow and blanket and a place on the divan. Rose said he intended to depart Bonaventure the next morning, and none raised an eyebrow that an associate of the farm's founder might be granted a free night's room and board. Yet even so, something about tiptoeing past the parlor made Minerva uneasy; and for some ambiguous reason, she felt that Rose's ears would prickle at the sound of her sneaking toward the kitchen door. Either instance, she was sure, would lead to inquiries and interrogation.

So instead, with great caution and stealth, she skulked to the open window at the end of the second-floor hall, climbed through and down the trellis, and stole across the yard.

The moon was half coming or going, Minerva didn't know which, but the result was that under a clear sky she had little need of a lantern anyway. The road past the fields and cabins glowed beneath her lace-up boots, even after it trickled into two ruts between weeds. Soon the woods closed over her head, shielding her from the moonlight, and she slowed her pace, wondering if she might lose the path and stray off into the thickets. Strangely, the thought of another pit failed to frighten her. Then the black hulk of the stone house rose on her right, elevated slightly from the road, the windows blank and dark. Carefully she swung herself up the incline, using the skinny maples and birches like walking canes to prevent her from tripping.

For a long moment she stood on the step. In her bed Minerva hadn't conceived how this moment should go. It was entirely possible Lyman was sound asleep and she might knock all night before he answered. And yet she asked herself if knocking was even proper. Tradition and niceties seemed superfluous in a world of moonlight and undefined space, like a landscape where the artist had run out of pigment before reaching the edges. Dupin wouldn't knock, *that* she was sure of.

The door was unlatched, the bolt unshod. It slid open on silent oiled hinges.

The main room was barely furnished, though the floor was swept and the windows shut. Cautiously she stumbled through the room to the mantel. A pair of stubby candles waited there, hard wax pooled in the dishes of their holders, but when she knelt to poke the ashes in the grate, she couldn't even find an ember to light them.

Perched on a corner of the stone was a piece of paper, dropped there as if the owner, having made reference to it, became distracted and laid it aside, forgotten. Immediately a vision of Sutton furiously jumping up from his afternoon coffee, letter in hand, lunged at her from the recesses. She seized the sheet and in less than four steps crossed to the window.

Yet peering close to it in the moonlight, Minerva apprehended it was not a letter at all.

Brothers and Sisters
evil
the Basement
to be
No one should go
picnic
lunch
yes/no
good Friend
hog, pig, swine

And thusly the list continued. The words and phrases were written in a neat and measured hand, arranged in columns of ten. Minerva quickly calculated over three-hundred seventy itemized.

"You haven't—why not—too long—"

As if lifting off the page in her hand, words floated up through the floorboards to Minerva's ears. They arrived as incomplete fragments, chopped and sawed, without meaning. Though distant and far away, yet Minerva recognized the voice unmistakably as Lyman's. Yet whom he spoke to, if anyone, Minerva could not distinguish.

She dropped the list back onto the mantel, the paper again forgotten, and breathed deeply. Carefully she stepped across the floorboards, allowing only the leather of her sole and never the heel to touch wood. The basement door stood wide open, a black portal gaping in deep shadow; and Minerva regretted being unable to light the candles from the mantel. Yet she told herself whatever advantage of sight it provided would negate stealth; and so, very carefully, with hands on the rail, she dipped her toe over the edge of the landing, seeking the step below; and when that was found, lowered herself by slow inches onto it before reaching out for the next.

"I cannot—you demand—"

By careful descent Minerva found herself in the basement, wrapped in thick blackness. She turned and saw, from beneath the stairs, a soft glow coloring the mouth of a low tunnel. The earthen floor made movement easier, muffling her steps, even if she fumbled in darkness as complete as a tomb's. Her hands trailed like those of a blind man's along the wood of the staircase, refusing to leave it behind, a single line of string leading her from the labyrinth. When she realized she could go no farther without releasing it, she held her breath and lunged at the tunnel entrance, only releasing the air from her lungs once the damp, cobwebby stone pressed against her palms.

Very little was clear to her: the short tunnel and, at the other end, a globe of lamplight illuminating a stage bereft of Lyman or any other player. As her perspective of the room was incomplete, Minerva reasoned they stood just out of view.

And yet from her vantage, she could now hear the second voice.

"May I remind you of the bargain the two of us struck."

Something about the pronunciation of those whispered words, so deep and heavy winded—almost *hissed*—sucked the breath from Minerva's lungs.

"I've already done so much for you. You don't even understand what you're asking," said Lyman. "Do you want more food? Another hog—"

"No more food. That would be tedious."

Mr. Sutton's John Tyler. Here was a conundrum solved—true to Sutton's suspicions, the animal *had* been stolen and butchered. But in the solution lay a thousand more dubieties.

Minerva heard a sound like muffled thrashing. "I can't do anything like this."

The other voice did not respond. In the silence, Minerva felt every grain of earth beneath her feet grinding like millstones, ready to betray her.

"I confess, it gladdened me a little to hear what he said. Your appetite is so unchained, an abundance of your kind would be a plague upon the earth." Lyman's tone held a controlled spite. "I wonder, what did you eat before I came to Bonaventure? How did you survive?"

"We supped upon the venery of the greenwood."

Lyman grunted in dismissal. "There haven't been deer or animals in these woods for years—deserts have more life than this farm. No, you hunted the local game into oblivion long ago, or at least anything large enough to sustain you."

No reply.

"I'll ask again: What did you eat before I arrived? The farm sat uninhabited for decades. I can guess what Garrick did. But what of the years in-between?"

There was a long sigh. *"We supped upon each other."* Almost ashamed. *"Maid swallowed gammer, strong compeers supped weak compeers. We separated, each to herself. Until the end."*

"And you are the last."

"We are the strong."

Nothing about the sibilant voice metamorphosed except its diction. As a draft horse pulls a plow and then a cart without altering its gait, the voice's cadence and pronunciation were unaltered. Only its grammar regressed, its vocabulary suddenly becoming almost Biblical, like a fire-and-brimstone preacher who, having read too much scripture, adopted the King James eloquence for his own sermons.

"So why not leave here and go where you can hunt? Why do you stay?"

The other voice didn't answer immediately. *"We came hither to sup. For many twelvemonth the supping was good. 'Struth, but we delved too many tunnels. Too many crumbled. The bowlders shifted and hereupon we were insnared."*

Lyman said, "So why leave now? Is it because —"

"We are your compeer. No scaramouch we are. Mr. Doyle and Mr. Myerson, you remember. May I remind you of the bargain."

"What do you think I can do against them? You're asking for *me* to defend *you* when —"

Suddenly a breeze blew down the tunnel onto Minerva's face, the air sulfurous and rotten. Lyman swore and an instant later the entire basement shook under Minerva's feet as if the ceiling dropped onto the floor.

"You now own a full share in our *enterprise."* Louder and clearer, the voice much closer than before, its diction once again changing, reversing from the ancient to the modern. *"If you don't, we're going to have to hurt I'm Minerva."*

Minerva jammed her hand into her pocket, squeezing the

medallion in an effort to constrict the panic within her; and yet some small sound escaped her throat, some infant shriek strangled in its crib.

"I agree!" Lyman's voice rose almost hysterically. "I will do as you demand—just, please. I beg of you. *Please.*"

In the other cellar, something scraped and flailed, then withdrew. A long moment of silence stretched over the basement as if the two speakers considered each other. In those seconds Minerva became convinced she had been overheard—the pounding of her heart and blood would alert a deaf man.

"You're leaving?" said Lyman, cooler now. "How am I supposed to help like this? Who will free me?"

There was long snarl, a grumbled note of threat. "*Who will free me.*" The words repeated but the emphasis altered.

"What's that supposed to mean?"

No answer came. A scrabbling noise recessed into silence.

The window of her eavesdropping was closing, Minerva knew, the sash nearly at the sill. Now was the moment to retreat softly toward the stairs and up and out of the house—and yet iron weighed her limbs and each foot was shod in lead. The lamplight in the other room flickered upon the brick.

Yet no one approached. She heard more of the soft thrashing, then panting breath.

Minerva crept glacial inches into the shadows beyond the tunnel mouth, stopping to listen. When she heard silence, she continued, and by slow measures passed through the tunnel. Like a mouse nosing from its hole, she peeked around the corner into the dome-shaped room.

She saw the open mouth of the cistern and the lamp beside it, its oil burning low. And beside that lay Tom Lyman, alone and unaccompanied by any other speaker, staring straight back at her, his hands and ankles bound with rope.

CHAPTER THREE

After breakfast David Grosvenor, scarf wound tight about his throat, passed through the kitchen on his way to the door. He kissed his wife on the cheek as she bent over the stove, beginning her long day's labor of canning the green beans from the garden. Retta and Nancy wiped and sorted the empty jars on the tabletop. From the cellar emerged little Tilly, running yesterday's jars to the shelves below, where she arranged them like chessmen beneath the bags of carrots and onions hanging from nails in the floor joists.

"Mind you don't bump your head," he said to her.

The young woman laughed. "I've a few inches to spare," she said, waving to the empty space above her.

Outside, Kit stacked firewood from the hand cart along the back wall of the house. "Morning, David!"

David breathed deep on the stoop. "A good morning to you, Kit. What a fine day."

"I reckon it will be warmer this afternoon, with no rain."

"I reckon you're right." Grosvenor hopped down the short flight and left him to his stacking.

As he passed the barn, he waved to Bart and Ned, busy at replacing a few boards rotted at the bottom. Brushes and a bucket of paint beside them spelled out the course of their day. Over by the chicken coop, he offered another wave to Flossie as she scattered dried corn among an audience of impatient hens. She smiled and would've returned the greeting had her hands not been full.

In the field along the road, Mal and Virgil and Lena mowed with their scythes, binding the cut grass into sheaves. "Hello, David," they called as he walked.

"Hello, hello!"

Farther, Presley and a handful of men worked clearing a patch of never-used soil, digging at stumps or piling rocks into a second cart. Bessie chewed thoughtfully nearby, waiting to be hitched to a stump sufficiently exposed to daylight. Come spring, Bonaventure would have that much more land to till.

"Good morning!" Waves all around.

On the edge of the woods, Abe and Judah each had their hands on a crosscut saw, bucking a fallen timber into eighteen-inch lengths. Nearby lay a splitter and a mound of quartered logs.

"I just saw Kit," said Grosvenor to them. "He should be along shortly to refill his cart."

"Tell him not to hurry," said Judah as he wiped a handkerchief across his face.

Grosvenor chuckled and nodded before plunging into the trees.

Within the half-hour, David Grosvenor clambered over a boulder field, the heat of the exercise canceling the coldness of the morning. Already his fingers, numb from the long walk through the woods, warmed with blood as he grabbed and gripped his way across. It was the most barren corner of his farm, that place, the rocks of every size pushed into one wide mound by ice and by time. As always, it was as lifeless and silent as a mausoleum.

His earlier mood of camaraderie deserted him. Unlike previous visits, dread shadowed this morning's arrival to the field, echoing its utter bleakness. He recalled Emerson: *Nature always wears the colors of the spirit*. Grosvenor's very first exploratory hike to the place had been driven by simple curiosity, by a desire to learn more about the property. There had been subtle hints in some of the property's papers obtained during the acquisition—suggestions about a graveyard, or the fact that the death of Sed Garrick had never been confirmed by anyone outside the family. That emotion of mystery had been transmuted to wonder and awe by what he'd discovered among the rocks and boulders; and subsequently he always returned with excited anticipation, the same feeling experienced when reading a book he couldn't set down. For two years he had read the book, learning, ruminating, applying what wisdom he gleaned to Bonaventure and its success—or at least toward keeping it from total failure. Today he reached the back cover.

For the moment he satisfied himself with not breaking a leg or twisting an ankle as he hopped and scrabbled over the rocks to the field's epicenter, where the terrain flattened into a kind of tabletop dotted by puddles of rainwater. Its centerpiece was a low cairn of smaller stones some seven or eight feet long. Grosvenor, after catching his breath, began to remove these smaller stones from the pile one at a time, placing them neatly aside. After the work of some minutes, cold sunlight fell upon the face of a granite statue buried beneath the stones.

Michelangelo would have envied the craftsmanship of the effigy, each hair of the beard and brow distinguished in stone, the lifelike wrinkles carved beside the nose and the corners of the mouth. Yet he might also have questioned the artist's choice of model, for the statue was not handsome; its face was overly oblong, and a sense of cruelty seemed etched into the wrinkles and hollow cheeks.

As Grosvenor placed the last stone beside the grave, he clapped the dust off his hands and inhaled the frosted air. "What a glorious morning to be alive," he said loudly.

The statue's eyes snapped open.

"Enjoy the dawn, Goodman Garrick," said Grosvenor, "for I'm afraid it's your last."

Like arrowheads the statue's blue eyes pierced the man standing over it. The lips trembled but refused to separate, as if sealed by glue.

Then by slow solvency they parted and a voice like grinding gravel spoke.

"As I am betrayed, so too shall thou be betrayed."

"Perhaps," said Grosvenor. He sat down on the seat of stones he had manufactured from the cairn. Grosvenor had never hinted at duplicity, had never suggested the thing he was about to do to Garrick; and yet Garrick's shrewd reading of Grosvenor's intent didn't surprise him. He and Garrick had never minced words—Sed Garrick, nearly calcified, could hardly spare the effort. Neither had they ever apologized for the things they'd done. Or, in Grosvenor's case, would do.

"I ask you, though," said Grosvenor, "is this existence so precious to you? I see myself as doing you a favor."

"Altruism is foreign to thy soul," said the statue with glacial patience. "Thou destroyest me to prevent anyone else from finding me as thou didst. To silence me."

"There's some truth in that. Yet ultimately, I act for Bonaventure's success, which is itself an altruistic act. What I have built will be remembered as a lighthouse in the sea of a dark age."

"Whatever thou hast constructed is for thy vanity alone. This trifle of thine will fail and in failing, be forgotten."

"I disagree. The gold your pet has brought me from underground was real enough. It has sustained Bonaventure this long—and will continue to, long after the beast has died."

"Only a fool would believe its serpent's mouth, but what care have I? Through it I will be revenged."

"I don't have to believe it," said a stern Grosvenor. "I didn't believe it at first. *I shall give thee what thou most craves*, it said. Gold in New England! Whoever heard of such a thing? But then I remembered stories of gold found in Litchfield County and sometimes panned in the rivers. It makes a kind of sense. The whole of Connecticut is like this," he waved his hands at the rocks around them, "with merely a plaster coat of topsoil above. If only something could dive beneath the stone, like a whale plunging into the abyss to pluck some treasure from the sea bottom."

Garrick was silent, as was his natural state.

"Do not forget it still needs me. If it expects to get what it wants then it will have to trust me. "Grosvenor regarded Garrick, still half buried in his crude sepulcher. "Mine is a simple transaction, *quid pro quo*. Your fault lay in asking the impossible. *I shall give thee what thou most craves*. And you answered, *immortality*." He shook his head.

"Thou thinkst thou understand it better than I do?" Garrick asked. "It delights in its own cleverness. To it there is no difference between boring through earth or boring through a man's mind. When thou art smote like its tunnels at daybreak, it will take pride at its work."

Grosvenor chuckled. "You are nothing if not persistent in your estimation of it. It's a dumb animal, nothing more. As a hound retrieves a pheasant from the brush, so has it retrieved my reward from deep below. Just as it retrieved the carbuncles that made you what you are today, I might add. But enough." Grosvenor stood. "I will miss our little debates. There is nothing left you can teach me and yet there's much harm you could still do, so we must bid farewell. My apprenticeship is concluded." He bent to pick up one of the larger stones he had been squatting upon.

"And the lives of those thee imperil? Thou thinkst nothing of them?"

"Why should I when the lives of those already devoured fail to bother me? They fulfill a greater intention—the realization of Bonaventure. No one among those living in the new house will ever bother to mourn those who died erecting its foundation." Grosvenor hefted the rock in his hands. "It's a little rich for you to counsel regret considering your own actions."

Something like a groan escaped Garrick's barely parted lips. "Perchance immortality has granted me time for it," he said softly.

"Well," said Grosvenor, "your time's run out."

With a roar he slammed the stone down on Garrick's skull, shattering both, but looking at the pieces afterward Grosvenor couldn't determine which was which.

◆ ◆ ◆

As Grosvenor and Isaac Rose turned the corner of the stone house, Lyman's hammer paused in mid-swing, hesitating over the head of a six-penny. His eyes studied Rose with a mix of alarm and suspicion, for the other man's expression contained little of the rugged good nature that had enamored Minerva. Lyman's voice, meanwhile, was silent, his lips otherwise preoccupied in pinching several nails between them.

"Ah, there you are," said Grosvenor. "Mr. Lyman, pleased to meet Mr. Rose."

"This is him, huh?" Rose asked Grosvenor.

"Yes," said Grosvenor, "I'm afraid so."

Lyman pulled the nails from his mouth. "What—"

Rose socked Lyman fast in the left eye. Lyman sprawled to the ground.

Lyman rolled on the ground a moment, holding his face and cursing.

"Listen to the yap on him," said Rose. "I've long believed swearing is a sign of weak character. Here's proof."

Grosvenor watched in disgust and distaste, as if Lyman's injury was a contagion. "Was that really necessary? You said nothing of violence."

"I do apologize," said Rose, "but I must remind you that my business associates are missing and I believe Caleb here has some knowledge of it."

Rose leaned down and grabbed Lyman by the shirt collar, pulling him to his feet, then shoved him against the wall. "Where are Misters Myerson and Doyle? Tell me, you little wood rat."

Lyman held his empty palms up, squinting at Rose through his one good eye. "It's all right, don't hit me. You want the money—I'll give you the money. It's in the basement."

"I don't want just the money," said Rose. "Where are the other two? There's no way a scrubby runt like you could've squared off against them."

"I'll show you. The money is in the basement. Let's all go to the basement."

"He may have buried it down there," said Grosvenor. "I scoured the house not long after his arrival but couldn't find it."

Lyman glared at him but Grosvenor only shrugged. "A thief has no right to complain about burglary."

Rose half-carried, half-pushed Lyman ahead of him, his forearm wrapped against Lyman's throat, into the house and down the stairs and through the tunnel to the cistern room. All the while Rose's attention stayed sharp for tricks or booby traps or hidden weapons. Grosvenor shuffled behind, carrying a pair of lamps.

Lyman pointed toward the open cistern. "It's in there," he said, "hanging from the top rung."

Rose, after confirming the room was empty of weapons or escape routes, threw Lyman to the dirt floor. He cautiously leaned over the side of the pit.

"Well, I'll be. There's a bag hanging here." Rose grabbed the rope and began pulling it up hand over hand.

The ends of Rose's hair danced. Softly at first and then with growing intensity, a breeze blew up the cistern and through the room. Rose stopped his reeling and stood frozen, almost mesmerized. Something far off rumbled, growing louder.

Grosvenor dropped the lanterns and grabbed Rose by the shoulder. "Get back."

With a sound like splitting timber, a great pale monstrosity lunged over the edge of the cistern, its snapping jaws seizing the empty space where Rose had been a second before. It landed on the basement floor, half in and half out of the hole, swinging its reptilian maw like a scythe.

With a high-pitched shriek, Rose drew a caplock pistol from his coat, but Grosvenor grasped his wrist and pushed it toward the ceiling while waving his other hand in front of the beast's snout.

"Stop! Do not attack!"

The thing regarded Grosvenor with shiny black eyes little bigger than pinheads.

"There is no food here. Return to your pit."

A baritone growl rolled in its throat.

"Go, I said."

Slowly with its spade-like claws it pushed itself backwards, its sinuous bulk receding into the cistern. Just before its jaws passed the rim, it looked straight at Rose.

"*Another new recruit.*"

Then it slid and scrabbled away and was gone.

Once Grosvenor was sure the wild-eyed Rose had regained control of his instincts, he released the man's wrist. Rose lowered his arm but refused to holster his weapon.

Lyman, meanwhile, had pushed himself to a sitting position against the wall. He studied Grosvenor with a steely glare.

Rose began to babble questions: *What is it? How does it talk?* Grosvenor, for some minutes, expounded upon the nature of the thing they'd just now witnessed, including its conjectured origins, its behavior and intelligence, and its facility for speech. Certain specifics and details he left obscured. Lyman, by way of silent expressions that passed across his face, indicated he did not agree with Grosvenor on every point; and Grosvenor, observing these wordless criticisms of his lecture, felt a spike of irritation so severe it surprised even him. He wished Rose would hit Lyman again.

"But it listened to you," said Rose. "It obeyed you as would a hound."

"Precisely," said Grosvenor. "It is a stupid beast, easily controlled by sticks and carrots. I have it under my thumb."

"You trained it?"

"As a horse is broken, so I broke it."

"And yet you also say it dwells underground, tunneling like a mole."

"Yes."

"Might not it be used to fetch as a dog fetches?"

Grosvenor answered with pretended indifference. "Perhaps."

"It occurs to me there might be some use for such a beast," said Rose. "I grew up not far from Dahlonega in northern Georgia. You've heard of it?"

"Of course," said Grosvenor in an uneasy tone. The town had been the nexus of a gold rush less than two decades before; the hills were so fertile with the stuff that the U.S. Mint had opened a branch office in

Dahlonega to strike coins.

"Most of the gold around Dahlonega is played out," Rose said. "As a result, many of the old claims considered exhausted can be bought cheap. If someone were to buy up some deeds and then have a fresh go at them with this trained mole of yours, who knows what wealth it could uncover."

Grosvenor shook his head. "Unfortunately, the creature you saw is old and too large to transport so far a distance."

"Are there any more of them?"

"I'm afraid it's the last of its kind."

Lyman said, "It's pregnant."

Like the shadow of some maleficent sundial, Grosvenor's head rotated slowly to cast Lyman into the darkness of his stare.

Rose laughed. "Well now boy, is that a fact?"

"It is," said Lyman. "It's preparing to lay its eggs soon." He sat with one hand over his swelling eye, the rest of him loose and ready like a hawk on tree branch, observing events below, waiting.

"It's easier to train a pup than a toothless hound. Is what he says true, Mr. Grosvenor?"

Grosvenor mumbled something.

"Say again? I didn't catch that."

"Yes," said Grosvenor louder, "I believe Mr. Lyman to be correct."

"But, Mr. Grosvenor, didn't you just say it's the last of its kind?" The easygoing malice, so recently directed toward Lyman, now focused on the other man. "Forgive me, but didn't it take Adam *and* Eve to make Cain and Abel?"

Grosvenor took a deep breath. "Yes, but it's a matter of *when*. A child gestates in the course of forty weeks. But the gestation of an elephant is nearly two years. A whale is almost as long. For an animal as ancient as this, who can say? Forty years, forty decades, maybe. Regardless, the male is long dead."

Lyman said, "As far as you know," but neither of the other men acknowledged him.

"Mr. Rose," said Grosvenor, "I'm sorry to have given you a fright with an appearance of our local wildlife, but may I remind you of the bargain the two of us struck not more than an hour ago in my office. You are to remove this—" he pointed at Lyman "— this *criminal* from Bonaventure henceforth and take him to New York for justice, and in return for leading you to him, I am owed a finder's fee of twenty percent of any monies found in his possession."

"I take it our arrangement of an extra twenty dollars a month is voided," said Lyman.

Grosvenor regarded him coolly. "Why settle for an annuity when the principal can be withdrawn as a lump sum?"

"Of course. But I'm curious. Am I the only one with whom you've made a special arrangement at Bonaventure?"

"I will put it to you this way, Mr. Lyman," said Grosvenor. "You may be something special to my daughter, but you're nothing special to *me*."

Rose walked over to the cistern and pulled up the rope with the bag at the end. He dashed away from the edge before opening the bag. His examination produced a low whistle.

"I am a man of my word, Mr. Grosvenor," said Rose. "I'll give you your twenty percent. However, I should add that my employer, Mrs. Tallmadge, has stated that, as an incentive, whomever locates Caleb may keep his stolen money as reward, which means I now possess the remaining eighty percent." Rose held up the bag. "It therefore appears I am in a position to purchase some of the eggs of this strange turkey you've been growing here on your farm."

"That's quite out of the question." Grosvenor's voice trembled.

Rose fingered his pistol and said to him, "I'm not asking any question."

Grosvenor awoke from his first sleep and lay listening. His wife breathed softly beside him; the house silent save for the typical creaks. Checking his pocket watch on the nightstand was impossible in the inky darkness, but he judged the hour past midnight. He pecked his wife on the forehead, rose, and dressed.

Downstairs, as soon as Grosvenor touched the floorboards, Rose threw off the blanket and sat up on the small couch in the parlor. Something inside Grosvenor sank.

The yard under a new moon was just as impenetrable as indoors, and only the light of the men's half-hooded lantern illuminated the clouds of frosty breath as they puffed their way to the stone house, with a short pause at the toolshed for Grosvenor to retrieve a rucksack. They walked in silence, cautious of being overheard by some insomniac farm member, the gravel of the road crunching beneath their soles. Grosvenor turned back toward the Consulate, and with relief saw neither light nor curious face at any window. Slowly, in a long exhale, he released the air in his lungs.

The stone house loomed blacker than the black night. In the basement they found the well room dark and empty. On the ground lay the rope Rose had used to bind Lyman's wrists and ankles.

"Our hen has flown its coop," said Rose. "He's probably miles from here. Now I have to hunt him down again."

"You already have his money," said Grosvenor. "The bounty will wait." He dangled his lantern over the edge of the well, peering into the depths. "Though I do wish he had left the extra lamp." His voice betrayed a certain misgiving for what would come next.

Rose also stared with reluctance into the pit. "How do you know it's not down there? Waiting for us?"

"It's gone. It could wait no longer."

"But how do you *know?*"

In truth Grosvenor knew little but intuited much. Its slyness was uncanny, he admitted. It was easy to see how Garrick could attribute intelligence to it, to credit its instinctual navigation of matters both conjectural and practical. Yet always upon reflection, nothing in its behavior or words struck him as originating from anything other than a very smart dog, assuming dogs could speak. A dog was fawning and servile. The thing—it had no proper name, and so Grosvenor always thought of it as just *the thing*—had a knack for ingratiation, for knowing just how to present itself. It wanted to please its master and therefore fetched or herded or ratted according to breed; the benefit to man seemed purposeful but was merely a consequence of the dog's desire for scraps or a spot by the hearth. Whatever cunning it displayed was illusory.

Grosvenor said in reply, "If it wanted us, it could have taken us the instant we walked out of the Consulate door. It would've heard our footsteps across the porch and down the stairs. Even now it would know exactly where we stand, were it still on the farm."

"Its hearing is that good?"

"Believe me, Mr. Rose—it hears *everything*."

With nothing else to be said, they descended the ladder to the floor of the pit. Grosvenor did his best to ignore the muck that littered it and the suggestions in its odors and shapes. Instead he waved his lantern in the mouths of the various passages. Finally he chose one tunnel, which seemed smoother and cleaner than the others, and ducking his head, led the way down its course.

They did not travel far when something glittered under the lamp's beams.

Grosvenor stepped forward and picked up the raw nugget, held it close to his face. He judged it near twenty-two karat purity—it was no pyrite—and weighing close to three pounds. By far the largest yet, worth at least nine hundred dollars.

The things Grosvenor could do with that money.

Rose let out one of his whistles and held up his lantern to see it. "You mean to say your creature leaves gold laying around here like pennies at the beach? You're right, Mr. Grosvenor—that animal is worth something."

Quickly the nugget vanished inside Grosvenor's deepest coat pocket. He knew the first thing anyone wants when unexpected money is received is a percentage.

"No, Mr. Rose," he said. "It never leaves such things by accident. What you saw just now was a small token left here on purpose, intended to be found by me alone." *As a cat leaves a dead sparrow on the doorstep,* Grosvenor thought. A parting gift left for its master, whom it imagined it would never see again.

Or was it something else? Perhaps it suspected Grosvenor would follow it—perhaps it intuited the dark errand Grosvenor was on. A bribe, a dissuasion from further harassment. A payoff.

But this was attributing too much to it. Grosvenor considered the attack on Minerva and Judith earlier in the day; he knew to ascribe logic to an animal was itself irrational. The girls had simply been in the wrong place at the wrong hour. The appetence that seized it, the passion of what every fiber drove it to do, only made the creature more bestial than ever. Grosvenor was the one who wielded carrots and sticks, not the animal.

The possibility of a third interpretation of the gold never entered Grosvenor's mind.

The tunnel ran as crooked as a nightcrawler pulled from under a log, and often they arrived at crossroads where other passages crossed the main before curving into shadow. Many of these lay either partially or completely collapsed, making the decision of which course to take easy; and in cases when it wasn't, Grosvenor always selected the smoother bored of the choices, reasoning that these were more trafficked by their quarry and therefore more stable.

As they walked—or rather staggered, both men having to stoop as if in a low-ceilinged cellar—Grosvenor endeavored to keep his mind from thinking too much about the confined arteries they traveled. He began to babble. He identified the composition of protruding rocks, he noted the strata of the soil. He soon digressed into the phenomenon of the Moodus Noises, explaining how they resulted from tunnels dug by the beast that collapsed after its passage through them—an infelicitous topic, considering their circumstance.

"This is why the beast could never leave the farm by tunneling," Grosvenor said, "for the whole is surrounded by a ring of rock too precarious and dense for it to penetrate. That's why it must travel aboveground to escape."

"But why couldn't it do that before?" Rose massaged his lower back with a free hand, sore from the bending. "Why *tonight?*"

Arrived at another nexus, Grosvenor chewed his lip before plunging forward. "Doubtless you've heard tales of a man dying and his dog waiting patiently on the doorstep for him to come home. The two situations are similar. Today the last leash tethering the beast was —"

His sentence went unfinished. In that instant, collapsing dirt and gravel echoed somewhere close. Both men halted suddenly.

"Your pet's behind us." Rose's voice was a whisper.

"No. It's the tunnel crumbling. We must hurry."

They continued on, thoughts of premature burial hastening their steps. Their course, which did not always keep to the horizontal, began a deep decline. Rocks and clods slid before them as they scudded down the slope, and the weight of the earth above them burdened their minds like chains. In the lamplight sweat ran down their faces, the air as humid and thick as the closing walls. They halted again at the clatter of rolling rock and showering sand.

"I tell you, something's following us."

Grosvenor shook his head, wheezing, the air almost too solid to breathe.

Neither voiced their mutual fear, which was the dread vision of rounding a turn only to find the way blocked, forcing them to follow their own steps backwards only to find it collapsed, trapping them. Not soon enough their path struck an upwards tack. The walls sped by, coarse and freshly dug, uninterrupted by cross-passage or byway, and then suddenly they scrabbled up a near vertical length and over the rim like clumsy swimmers pulling themselves over the gunwales of a boat. In the cold night air, the sweat turned to ice on their faces, and both realized they had been running.

Still huffing, they picked up the trail again. It wasn't hard to find. The creature's weight and claws had carved deep rents and fissures into the soil, and following its path through the trees and across the roads was like following in the path of a narrow tornado, the earth disrupted and altered by its transit.

Rose seemed content not to speak or ask questions. With the pressure of tons above them removed, conversation was now the last thing Grosvenor desired. With a deep breath he reminded himself that soon he'd be rid of the beast forever. It was a leftover, a remnant of Sed Garrick, and with Garrick gone, the last of his tools would soon follow.

The generation that came next—they would be *Grosvenor's* tools.

By the use of side lanes and meanders, the trackers bypassed Saltonstall and kept to the loneliest roads and woodlands, passing darkened farmhouses and fields through November air as sharp as shears. They kept the lantern wicks dialed low.

The miles passed quickly as they followed the path of ruin over the landscape.

In lockstep beside Grosvenor, Rose walked with jaw clenched, the muscles of his back and shoulders tauter than a hangman's knot. If one's initial encounter with a bear involves nearly being savaged by it, then he may be excused for feeling some anxiety as he sets out in search of its cubs. Part of Grosvenor wished the thing had finished Rose in the basement; and another part daydreamed of it rising up with a roar to send Rose scampering into the night. If the bounty man had just taken Lyman and gone, that would've been the end of it. Now, their arrangement was more—complicated.

And yet as they walked, something crept to the forefront of Grosvenor's attention, like shadows in the corner of the eye that are dismissed as nothing, yet gradually grow into awareness. It was the conviction they were not alone. More than twice Grosvenor happened to glance into the trees behind him to see a brief dot of light as of a hastily covered lantern or shapes in the night that suggested skulking figures. When he blinked to look again, he saw only darkness broken by trunks and undergrowth. His mind attributed these distractions to tiredness and the gravity of his errand, to the fear of being discovered.

Except Rose saw it too.

"Hold on," he said. Rose handed Grosvenor his lantern and vanished among the wildness. A moment later there was a shout and Grosvenor thought he heard a woman's voice. Then silence.

Finally, Rose reappeared, his pistol pointed at the backs of two figures who marched before him. Minerva and Tom Lyman.

Grosvenor's shock was apparent. "How now," he said to them, "my sweet child, what are you doing so far from your bed at this hour? And Mr. Lyman, what villainy is this?"

Drawn and white, Minerva ignored his question. "Father, better to ask your conscience what brings *you* here."

Grosvenor addressed Lyman. "You are a devil of a man. What thoughts have you placed into her head to bring her to some lonely hilltop so early in the morning? You, sir, are no better than a kidnapper."

But Lyman, resolute, shook his head. "I believe we'll return to our blankets the quicker without obfuscations or diversions. We know your errand."

During this intercourse, Rose had fished a length of rope from his pocket—the same used on Lyman earlier. "Well," Rose said, "if we all agree what we're doing here, let's get on and be done with it," and he wound and tied an end around Minerva's wrists and the other around Lyman's, leaving them bound and connected by a length of several feet.

"Mr. Rose," said Grosvenor, "unhand my daughter. She is not one of your criminals to be tethered to a chain gang."

"To be sure I will, as soon as I get what I came for."

Grosvenor's face reddened. "You dare take my own blood as hostage? You're suddenly too brash."

"Is that a fact?"

The two men stared at each other—but there is little contest when only one among them holds a pistol. Instead Grosvenor turned toward his daughter, the demand for an explanation insistent. Minerva stood straight and silent, facing forward.

"How do you come to be here?" Grosvenor asked her. "It was you following us through the tunnels. How did you know?"

"How indeed," she said. But the answer to the first question was simply this: she and Lyman were much practiced walkers.

"More moving the feet," said Rose, "and less moving your gums." He shoved Lyman forward.

The group resumed in funereal silence. The trail soon led to a road, which they followed another half-mile. Grosvenor became dimly aware of a distant crashing of breakers on the shore when Rose pointed up a pine-covered hillside.

Tracking its upwards course was effortless: the furrows hewed by it bulk and the bark scraped from the trunks blazed a trail for blind men. The slope, mild at first, inclined quickly, and under the glow of their lanterns and the dappling moonlight the great divots clawed by its mole-like nails grew in number and depth. Gradually it had made its way uphill through the orange needles and the dead lower branches of towering white pines.

As they crested the hill, the volume of the waves increased. The trail vanished. Frantically Grosvenor waved his lantern high, worried their quarry might have escaped into subterranean safety before entering its throes.

And then they noted the slope below them, where the ground leveled flat before descending again toward the Sound. In the flashing beams, they saw the earth torn and loose, and in its center, surrounded by a berm like a crater, lay a dozen melon-sized globes with speckled shells.

There was no intimation of where their creator had gone.

"I had expected them to be buried, as reptiles will do," said Grosvenor. "But here they await us openly, like sprouting fruit." He turned to Rose. "Take your egg, as agreed, as well as your man, and go."

Rose didn't budge. "Thank you, Mr. Grosvenor. I'd be happy to oblige except for one thing. It occurs to me that in any litter, there's always a runt. How do I know this egg isn't a runt?"

"I cannot warranty anything," said Grosvenor. "You may take whichever egg you prefer. We must hurry." He surveyed the surrounding woods in anxiety. Somewhere out there, in the night, the thing was helpless from its ordeal—but as with the other factors, he could not guarantee for how long.

"Well now," said Rose, "it's difficult to choose one egg from another. I mean, when you're raising and training pups, you need to take the pick of the whole litter. But with hen's eggs, that decision can't be made until they're hatched. I believe I'm going to have to take them all to be sure."

The barrel of the pistol pointed toward Grosvenor's chest. "Oh," he added, "I'll be relieving you of that gold nugget too."

Grosvenor stood; fists balled at his sides. "You're nothing but a highwayman."

"I'm a lot of things, Mr. Grosvenor. And a rich man is what I intend to be."

Rose moved toward the clutch of eggs, pulling the rope connecting Minerva and Lyman. Impulsively Grosvenor lurched to interject himself.

Too late he noticed the insidious ring around the eggs. The soil there, more air than earth, dissolved beneath their soles, and like driven stakes the four dropped straight into the ground. Rose's pistol flew away and the lantern spilled. The surrounding dirt raced to fill the vacuum around their bodies, pinning them tight.

For some minutes each of them struggled and shouted, trapped in their personal oubliettes. The three men wriggled desperately, their arms trapped at their sides, chins level with the eggs, three throats shouting a chorus compounded into a medicine of nonsense. Only Minerva made any advance, for she had thrown up her hands over her head as she fell. As her wrists were bound, she had little success digging, and instead only progressed by thrusting her elbows into the dirt before her and shimmying upwards by scant inches before resetting and repeating. In her palms she still held Bitty's medallion, which she had carried with her the whole night.

She was the first to hear the scratching. She froze, leaning all her attention toward that sound, and one by one the others likewise halted as they grew aware of the insistent chipping noise.

Among the clutch, an egg cracked and a piece of the shell tore off. A reptilian beak poked out.

How clever is the trap, Minerva wondered just then, when the wolf doesn't even realize he's been caught? No ruse is more cunning than the one in which the flimflammed doesn't recognize the swindle. For just as the artist's character might be intuited by scrutinizing the brushstrokes and composition of his paintings, so too the transcendentalists believed something of God's nature could be intuited by studying His Creation.

Yet in turn they were studied as well, except not by God. It occurred to Minerva they were understood by their deeds and their actions and, most of all, by their words. Each of them brought there to that precise place, at that specific time, lured by greed or ambition or indebtedness or threat. And Minerva, what had brought her there? Some combination of curiosity, love both daughterly and otherwise, and yes, suspicion—but there isn't a single sphinx's riddle in this world that wasn't untangled by suspicion. The bait varied by the fish, but each of them hooked nonetheless, and deposited on the riverbank.

To be eaten.

So consumed were they by the panic of the moment, none of the four understood their predicament until that firstborn hatchling slid from its slimy bed, full of claws and a hungry snapping mouth. It was joined by a second and a third, and within minutes only a singular egg remained intact. The mass of them yowled and snipped until finally they discovered the means of locomotion, and they crawled from their crib toward the milk provided them.

Deep beyond her vision, tumblers fell into place, each syllable like the tooth of a key, opening a lock. For a split-second Minerva felt an attention shifted onto her and her alone, and with rising dread she understood that focus to be equally malicious or benign according to its mood. Such was a tendency shared by everything on this planet—by beast and storm, by plant and stone—and which determined, often unpredictably and arbitrarily, whether we stood at the end of each day whole and successful or maimed and injured, or even dead.

Her initiation into the mystery was complete. "Hobomoko," Minerva said.

Free to the waist, Minerva leaned toward Lyman. She pressed Bitty's medallion into the earth, stamping the daisy wheel totem into the soil before him. She stretched and stamped the ground before her father.

Rose shook and thrashed at the earth about him, feverish for some purchase, but his arms remained imprisoned as if by chains. By slow measures the hatchlings descended upon him, blind to the other three. The first to reach him lashed savagely at his face, tearing off a long strip of his cheek. Another gouged his scalp. A third swiped off his nose in a single bite.

Rose howled. Minerva pushed and pulled her way free, and plunged her hands into the soil around Lyman, scooping and digging. In a moment his arms were extricated, and in another his whole body. Their efforts doubled, they freed Grosvenor twice as quickly. As she grabbed the lantern, Minerva glanced at Rose. Only his mouth was visible, opened wide to plead, or maybe scream, the rest of him buried beneath the pale maggoty bodies.

And then he did scream, louder than any heretic broken on a Spanish wheel, like nothing ever uttered by a human throat.

The Bonaventurists spilled and slipped their way down the hill, reckless and immune to bruises and knocks. More than once, the rope binding Lyman and Minerva caught on some tree or obstacle, and one or both of the pair fell, only to leap up immediately, disentangle, and resume their escape.

At the edge of the road, the trio paused to catch their wind and untie the rope and relight the single lantern that somehow escaped with them during their dash. Only then did Minerva observe what her father carried: slung over his shoulder, the rucksack brought from the toolshed contained the final unhatched egg.

She nearly grabbed him by his collar. "You cannot think to bring that—that *thing*—back to Bonaventure."

Grosvenor drew a deep breath. "Minerva," he said, "you must believe me when I tell you I can control it. Now it is but a formless yolk—but in time it can be trained, just as any beast. It can be disciplined. I will make it my instrument."

"Instrument for *what*? Murder?"

"For Bonaventure's success, of course. Think of it. Who needs men and oxen to waste their days plowing a field when one of these creatures can do it in minutes? Who need bother sinking a spade for a building foundation when it can do the task for us? And the gold, Minerva, I tell you—you cannot believe what lies beneath our feet—"

"And what will you raise this servant on? It doesn't subsist on carrots and onions."

"We can grow the hogs to feed it. In turn, it will labor for us just as Bessie does."

"You speak of the offspring. Yet what have you fed the parent during this time?"

Grosvenor shook his head. "The parent is redundant now and I cannot see an alternative to bringing the pup to Bonaventure. Should

I destroy it? Or would you have me risk my life to return the egg to its nest? To leave here in the wild, where it will hatch and grow into a ravenous monster that would plague the countryside?"

"I'm told there are lions in Africa," said Lyman, rubbing his naked wrists, "that occasionally will eat men. I cannot begrudge the lion for its character. I only insist it remain in Africa."

Minerva stepped closer. "Father," she said, "do you remember the morning we learned that Mr. Sutton departed the farm?"

Grosvenor snorted in exasperation. "Minerva, now is not the time for reminiscences. You must let it go."

"Who wrote the note nailed to the door?"

"Mr. Sutton, of course."

Minerva said, "Did you write it?"

"Minerva."

"Was it ever even nailed to the door? Or was the ink still drying as you read it aloud to us?"

Grosvenor looked at his daughter, an apparition of conscience manifested solidly before him, and felt a leaden yoke descend upon his shoulders.

"You're too young. You don't know what it is to fail." He gasped, trying to find words. "If Bonaventure fails, it's all anyone will talk about. It's how they'll remember it."

Lyman, who knew something about failure, felt the man's discomfort as his own. "We can leave the bag in the ditch," he said, "and just go."

"No," said Minerva. "He must answer my question first."

Grosvenor opened his lips to speak, and had an honest reply passed between them—whatever its content—a great deal of consolation would have assuaged his daughter's soul.

Yet at that moment there was a crack like thunder and a tree beside them burst into particles. Grosvenor, thinking to shield himself, leapt away, but the shape from beneath the road lunged straight for him.

The thing thrashed among the wreckage. Lyman grabbed a splinter of wood and jumped between it and Minerva, stabbing. With each successful piercing it squealed like a bow dragged across fiddle strings. Then its jaws caught the spar, pulling it from Lyman's grip to grind it into kindling. It exploded from the ruined tree, now just sticks and firewood, its tail swinging like a heavy chain. Lyman toppled backwards as it rushed past him, the sack in its mouth, to burst through a fieldstone wall into the pasture opposite the hill. Clods of earth flew in every direction, and with a rumble it was gone.

Lyman picked himself up, shaken, as Minerva raised the wick of the recovered lantern. She screamed.

Among the debris lay her father, his hips and legs twisted behind him, his spine bent forty-five degrees. Blood streamed from his face and he mouthed inaudible syllables, his eyes fixed on Minerva. The extent of his wounds was beyond him—in his gaze lay nothing except shock and confusion. He tried to crawl toward her in supplication but simply managed to spin himself in circles, like a coin accidentally dropped to the floor. Again, his lips opened and closed as if to impart some vital message, but the only issue was scarlet bubbles.

For a long moment the two of them witnessed this strange pantomime, Minerva shaking and sobbing. Then finally Lyman went over to the shattered wall and lifted a stone. Raising it high above him, he brought it down again to make himself a murderer twofold.

CHAPTER FOUR

The afternoon before the verdict was to be read, Minerva paid a visit. The constable stepped outside, and because the only other resident was a drunkard dead asleep, they had a measure of privacy.

"I hardly know how to address you," said Minerva through the bars. "Should I call you Tom, or by your other title?"

The briefest of smiles passed across his face. "I would like it very much if you called me by my Bonaventure name."

"Then I shall. Hello, Tom."

"Hello, Minerva."

Visitors were allowed to bring food to prisoners, and having passed inspection by the constable, she now handed the contents of a small basket through to him, hard-boiled eggs and apples and a small wedge of cheese. She explained each item as if he were a foreigner from some land where such produce didn't exist and Lyman listened carefully, knowing her words were uncontrollable waters that gushed from a broken dam. This was their first meeting since that night.

There then followed some obligatory questions about the conditions—the constable treated him well, he said; a few church ladies had come around from the meeting house to give him a blanket for the cold nights—and where he expected to be sent next. There was no question of how the jury would return. The sentence would be delivered immediately afterward and off he would be taken. A noose wasn't likely, not after Minerva and a string of Bonaventurists had paraded through the courtroom asking for leniency.

"I wanted to thank you, Tom, for not leaving me." She stared down at her clasped hands. "I think—I often think that you may not be in that cell if you had simply vanished into the night."

Lyman said, "It would have hurt you terribly if I did." He had thought about it, just slipping away. But what then? Where would he find some new Bonaventure to hide himself, to create a fresh repetition of damnation? Instead the local farmer who owned the broken stone wall, responding to the commotion, had found them in the road, Minerva in his arms, standing over a scene of death and ruin. Unlike some monsters, he couldn't just leave her there.

"That's true. I would have probably hated you for it. But at least you would be free, somewhere. I often daydream of that other life, and what it would be like, and if it would be better than this one. I feel it's something out of one of my novelettes."

When questioned by the judge, Minerva had stuck unerringly to the truth—*all* of it. And yet when it came to be Lyman's turn, the ridiculousness of it falling from his lips couldn't even convince himself. He gave little fight against the version of events delivered in the courtroom: about how he had followed Grosvenor and his daughter as they made their way under cover of deepest night to New London to sell the gold nugget found on the Grosvenor property; only instead of merely waylaying them on some lonely stretch of road without witness or interference, he had engineered their hypothetical wagon to crash into the wall, obliterating it completely, snapping Grosvenor's spine, and knocking Minerva senseless. Only after completing the job with a stone had Lyman been overcome with remorse at the sight of an addled

Minerva spouting nonsense and so surrendered himself to justice.

"I think yours," said Lyman, "is a common daydream. I often wonder how my life would've differed if I'd never entered that first error in Mr. Tallmadge's ledger and pocketed the difference."

Minerva said, "I tell myself again and again that any difference in action would likely produce the same result. And yet I cannot but wonder if I hadn't asked you to come with me, then my father—"

"Your request had nothing to do with the outcome. I would've gone anyway—I had already bet the devil my head, remember? It knew what your father planned with its eggs. It protected me from my hunters, and in repayment I was to thwart him. Neither of us could've predicted its true motives."

"It would seem as you stand behind those bars that consequences are what matter most."

"And yet your intent was laudable."

"My intent, once you told me what *he* intended, was to stop my father from returning to Bonaventure with the prizes he coveted. Instead, he failed to return at all."

Lyman was silent a moment and then said, "Having little else to think of, often I lie at night wondering if we should've returned up the hill and smashed them."

"Doing so would have opened you to vengeance."

"And I would not have dared any risk to you. As for me—" Lyman shrugged. "How many souls have we damned for the price of mine?"

Minerva said, "Emerson wrote that there are just two things: The Soul, and outside of it, Nature. Even the devil, therefore, is a thing of Nature."

The court, for reasons of its own, was reluctant to surrender the nugget of gold found in Grosvenor's pocket; yet eventually, after the grieving widow made several statements to the press that caused them embarrassment, they returned it. It was too little, too late. Upon sorting through Grosvenor's study, Minerva discovered—beneath books about animal migration and naturalist volumes authored by the likes of Georges Cuvier and Reverend William Conybeare and Charles Bonnet—her father's accounting ledgers. Bonaventure faced bankruptcy. The farm was subdivided and sold at auction, with the neighbor Whitney smugly picking up several choice acres. Likewise; the equipment, furniture, tools, and the rest, and Grosvenor's scientific collection of stones and books generated a few dollars, particularly an odd crocodilian skull discovered hidden behind a shelf. Between these proceeds, Minerva and her mother had enough left over to purchase a small home in New London where they lived comfortably, if modestly.

Bonaventure disbanded, each member going his or her own way. The Albys, after the birth of their son, joined a group of Shakers in Maine where Mrs. Alby rose quite high in the leadership. At the age of eighteen, Judith Alby left the colony and eventually became a renowned author—of *fiction*.

Presley moved to the former Fruitlands along with several survivors of that commune, where they attempted to make their livings as members of a commercial farm. Just before his departure, Mr. Presley sheepishly approached Minerva.

"I am a coward," he said to her. He was close to tears.

"Mr. Presley," said Minerva, "I can think of no word less fitting to describe you."

"It's true. That day you came to my cabin, I neglected to tell you something. It seemed trivial at the time, but after everything that's happened with Mr. Lyman, I don't know what to think."

"It can't have made any difference."

"I'm not so sure. Nonetheless I cannot leave Bonaventure without scrubbing my conscience."

"I understand."

Presley wrung his hands a moment more and then, without looking at her, said, "What I described to you about the final time I saw Mr. Sutton, I described truthfully. What I failed to tell you was that Mr. Sutton kept an amount of cash in his desk drawer, and when you explored his desk that afternoon, I noted the cash was missing. I naturally assumed he took it with him when he departed for New York."

Minerva considered. "Was Mr. Sutton wealthy?"

Presley's brow furrowed. "I don't know if *wealthy* is the proper word. But he did intimate on more than one occasion that he'd made several successful investments while working at the Exchange Board. It was a concern of his, how best to use the proceeds toward national abolition."

"And he kept some of it in his desk."

"Yes," said Presley. "I know so because I often saw him slip a banknote into the letters he sent to his sister in Pennsylvania."

"Show me."

Yet when they thoroughly searched the desk, they found not so much as a cent.

Presley's face flushed red. "I assumed he took the cash with him when he departed, but now—I assure you, I would never —"

"Of course not, Mr. Presley," said Minerva. "I would never accuse you of such a thing."

"He must've taken it with him," Presley repeated.

After a moment, Minerva said, "Was there anything unusual about Mr. Sutton the last time you saw him? I'd like to know, no matter how inconsequential it may seem."

Presley shook his head. "Nothing I can think of. As I told you, Mr. Sutton had received a letter from his friend in New York, and upon reading it, he jumped up suddenly and ran out of the cabin."

Deep inside Minerva, something tightened. "Did he say anything?"

Presley hesitated. "Yes, now that I think of it. He said, '*I must inform David of this.*' That was all."

Minerva kept her opinion to herself. Everyone attributed Minerva's account of what had transpired at Bonaventure to the concussion supposedly received from the wagon crash. She had found the more insistent she was, the less they believed her, about that and everything else.

Lyman was committed to the state prison at Wethersfield. In the beginning, he and Minerva corresponded frequently. The conditions were difficult at first, he wrote; but the men were expected to engage in trades for the support of the prison, and eventually Lyman was placed in the carpentry department, where he found some relief from his circumstances. The food was very basic. Still, Lyman complained little and these notes remained congenial if perhaps a bit self-conscious, considering the awkward relationship between the two authors.

Yet over time Lyman's letters became increasingly agitated. Originally Lyman's cell was located above-ground; but some months into his sentence he was transferred to a cell in the basement of the same building. Lyman refused to accept the transfer but ultimately was physically coerced, and all protests to the warden went ignored. This move had a deleterious effect on Lyman's nerves; he complained of being unable to sleep and, when he finally did, of being tormented by horrible dreams.

The letters abruptly ceased until December when Minerva received a short note in shaky handwriting. It pointedly requested that Minerva give him the leather medallion she had received from Bitty Breadsticks; he said she could think of it as a Christmas present. It had remained in her grasp during their flight down the hill and was returned to her pocket, but she'd thought no one else knew that fact. Lyman's brusqueness took her aback, but Minerva chose to remember her tender memories of him and did as he asked. He never received it: the medallion arrived at the prison—Lyman was told as much—but the officials refused to deliver it to him for arbitrary and indistinct excuses. Minerva wrote with indignation to the warden, demanding to know why her gift had not been delivered to the inmate. Some weeks later a response arrived in which the warden begged her forgiveness but explained that he did not feel it was in Lyman's best interests to give it to him. The medallion, as she well knew, was stamped with a daisy-wheel symbol with which Lyman had become obsessed, scratching it into the walls of his cell over and over with whatever implements he had at hand. When those implements were seized from him, Lyman would often knock his head against the wall, then use the resulting blood as ink to repeat the shape on the bricks.

After this, Lyman's letters degraded into hysteria. The last she received simply read,

Maybe they're not echoes Judith we must go back.

With a sorrowful heart, Minerva resolved to end her correspondence. The contents only reawakened unpleasant emotions, feelings of that long-ago autumn and especially that terrible night which she had learned to bury under the spadings of public disbelief. Better to leave them underground and settle into a common life.

Our experiences, so real and truthful to us, rarely translate adequately, if at all, to those around us, and so often it's easier to pack them away as old clothes in a trunk, out of view. Tell your friend you bought a load of groceries at the store and he will shrug, but tell him you've seen a ghost and he will laugh. People, like the stones in a partition between acres, may touch and rest upon one another, but ultimately each is a separate thing, alone and uncommunicative. Every stone believes its own story of how it came to rest there and only infrequently do those narratives overlap. Minerva was reminded of this years later when she read a newspaper report that the man she had known as Tom Lyman had escaped from incarceration at Wethersfield. Yet a closer reading of the story showed that escape was the reporter's assumption, while the warden himself, perhaps protective of his reputation, only admitted Lyman was missing.

What we encounter in the night we encounter by ourselves, whether it is murder, memory, violin music, or voices *plural*, whispering to us through prison walls.

FURTHER READING

Readers interested in learning more about transcendentalist utopian settlements may want to start with some of the semi-fictionalized testaments written by former residents. Nathaniel Hawthorne's *The Blithedale Romance*, inspired by his time at Brook Farm, is as dry and funny today as it was in 1852, and Louisa May Alcott's "Transcendental Wild Oats" (1873) is a satirical send-up of her father's experiment at Fruitlands.

I also suggest Ralph Waldo Emerson's essay "Nature" (1836) and Henry David Thoreau's "Walking" (1862) for understanding the transcendentalist mindset. Really, anything by Thoreau is recommended.

Philip F. Gura's *American Transcendentalism: A History* (2007) is a solid primer on transcendentalism in general. Finally, if you can find it, there is Edith Roelker Curtis's history of Brook Farm, *A Season in Utopia* (1961), now long out of print.

— JK

ABOUT THE AUTHOR

Jackson Kuhl is the author of the Revolutionary War biography *Samuel Smedley, Connecticut Privateer* and the fiction collection *The Dead Ride Fast*. Kuhl has written for Atlas Obscura, Connecticut Magazine, the Hartford Courant, National Geographic News, Reason, and other publications. He lives in coastal Connecticut.

For more information, visit www.jacksonkuhl.com.